tHE YEAR SHE LEFt

Kerry Kelly

darkstar fiction

Text © 2008 by Kerry Kelly

Cover art/design: Vasiliki Lenis/Emma Dolan
Author photo: Alex McKee

We acknowledge the support of the Canada Council for our publishing program.

We acknowledge the financial support of the Government of Canada through the Book Publishing Industry Development Program (BPIDP) for our publishing activities.

Darkstar Fiction
An imprint of Napoleon & Company
Toronto, Ontario, Canada
www.napoleonandcompany.com

Printed in Canada

12 11 10 09 08   5 4 3 2 1

Library and Archives Canada Cataloguing in Publication

Kelly, Kerry, date-
        The year she left / Kerry Kelly.

ISBN 978-1-894917-72-8

        I. Title.
PS8621.E4416Y42 2008   C813'.6   C2008-905619-1

For those about to rock

September

It was September when Stuart found out she was gone. Or rather, that he was going. He'd come home one day to find that Emily had left him a note on the kitchen table of their condo. Her condo. She'd made the down-payment.

Emily hadn't addressed him as "Dear". She told him later that she felt he deserved better than a cliché. He'd thought it unfortunate that she didn't think he deserved better than to be simultaneously dumped and evicted in a letter, especially after he found out that her decision to end things had actually been made months earlier. During a week he'd been out of town. On the day he was set to return. The day she had realized her engagement ring was missing.

She'd spent a whole day searching for it, starting with the obvious places; the nightstand, the soap dish and finally resorting to unhooking the bathroom drainpipe. But the ring was gone, and not even her prayers to St. Anthony were bringing it back.

It was a devastating loss; it was a beautiful ring, one sparkling karat riding high on a white-gold setting. Platinum was what you used to build missiles, she'd told him. She was vehemently opposed to warheads, and gold was more romantic anyway. Not gold-gold, though. It didn't suit her skin tone.

But that was not really why she was so upset. She was upset because she could not remember when exactly the little band of metal, rock and promise had slipped off her finger. It was a colleague who had brought it to her attention, asking her if she took it off when she typed.

As she said, "No, I always have it on," she realized she didn't. Her initial reaction was more curiosity than tragedy, until she saw the horrified expression on the other woman's face, a horror she then tried to mimic, rather unconvincingly.

She loved the ring. There was no reason she shouldn't have, since she was the one who had picked it out, shortly after their third anniversary. They had moved from their apartment into the condo she'd selected for them as well. Stuart had been a doll about it, telling her she had better taste than he did anyway, which was true, and that it was her money they were using for the downpayment, which was also true. She'd thought it was very modern of him to say so, not to feel threatened by her financial advantage.

She'd wanted to be engaged before they moved in, but she'd also wanted Stuart to pay for the ring. Some traditions had to be upheld. It had taken him longer than expected to scrounge up the money. Stuart had never really taken to a career. He had a degree in English Literature and a burning desire to be an artist. His painting never resulted in saleable pieces, just an unwillingness to get tied into some nine-to-five career that would make it impossible for him to focus on his true calling. He actually made his money designing websites for the companies of more successful family members and acquaintances.

When he did finally present her with the ring, they were at their favourite restaurant. He handed it to her in an antique ring box, looking up at her from bended knee, as per the orders Emily had given her best friend to give to him. It was perfect.

Until that day in late May, she had barely taken it off. In the very beginning, she hadn't wanted to wear it at night, since it tended to get caught in her expensive sheets and more expensively-styled hair, but he looked so wounded whenever he saw her slip it off that she'd started wearing it all of the time. Until...

She sat at her desk that day, trying to figure out when it had fallen off her hand. That morning, the evening before, the day before that? She had no idea.

As she tried to recall the last time she'd seen the ring, she had been a bit shocked to find that for all the months it had been a part of her, she couldn't really picture it on her finger. Couldn't quite remember what it would have looked like seeing it sitting there winking back at her.

She didn't have much time to think about it. From the corner of her eye, she could see Laurel, her colleague, watching for a more suitable reaction with an air of expectation

Emily dropped to her knees behind her desk in a move designed both to hide her from view and to show a genuine feminine upset that the ring was missing. As she crawled around, aimlessly patting the carpet, the thought of asking Laurel when she'd last seen the ring briefly crossed her mind. She'd obviously been keeping tabs on it. But Emily was too afraid to risk further gaping from someone who was already staring down at her with all the judgment of an Olympian god. Emily could feel it even through the solid maple of the desktop.

The fury of a woman scorned was absolutely nothing to that of one overlooked, any single woman could tell you that. And here was a woman who had been handed the proof that she was worth loving tossing that proof around like it was nothing.

She then toyed with the idea of bursting into tears. She was going to be fodder for the lunch-time gossip anyway, so it would be best to be portrayed in a favourable light, but she wasn't sure she could pull it off. Instead she stayed tucked under her desk, murmuring concerns and scratching at the pile of the rug until she heard the door click shut.

Grabbing her coat and keys, she headed for home. The hunt was on. She couldn't have been long without it, she reasoned. Stuart had only been gone a week, and she must have had it on when he left.

He would have noticed its absence. He had a tendency to stare at it, mesmerized, twisting it to see the sparkle. "This is how much I love you," he'd tell her, holding the hand up to better catch the light. It wasn't as gross as it sounded. Not really, though it had always made her cringe to hear it. It was just that Stuart was not a wealthy guy. For this purchase, he'd really buckled down, taking every job he could get and funneling all of the money he could into what he called the "Promise Fund". He'd given her everything the day he had proposed. The ring. A promise. His heart.

And she had gone and lost it. She'd shed it like a snakeskin and not even noticed. How could she tell him that? How could she ever explain it?

Once home, she began a panicked search of her condo. *Their* condo, she corrected herself. She was always having to correct herself. She started in the office, strewing papers and yanking on drawer handles. She did not find it.

In the bedroom, she checked in the sheets, then in the closet, kicking at shoes and digging through boxes she knew hadn't been touched in years. She did not find it.

She went from room to room like that, shoving and lifting and praying and calling out for his ring, his love, like a lost pup. "Where are you? Where the fuck are you?" She did not find it.

Hours later she sat, defeated, in a shirt smeared with drain sludge and with a handful of slivers, but without a ring. She was crying. She was crying because that was the day she finally admitted something that had been crawling around the back of her mind like an infection. That day was the day she told herself that it wasn't his love that was lost. It was hers. And everything was over.

How long had she known this? Like the ring, she couldn't pinpoint it. A few months? A year? The whole four years? No. Not that long. She had loved him once. She was sure that was true. She hoped to hell it was, but if she were honest, she knew that she hadn't felt that way in quite some time.

Did she love him when he'd asked her to move in? She thought so. When she'd bought the condo and not had him co-sign the lease? Maybe not. When he'd proposed?

No, she hadn't loved him when he'd proposed. But sitting in that restaurant with that gleaming silver box, she thought she ought to love him. It was what she'd asked for. And she'd seen how very much Stuart loved her. She just smiled, said yes and hoped he had enough love for both of them.

Sitting there that cool spring day, dirty and aching behind her eyes, she knew he didn't. She never should have expected it. She'd been unfair, and she'd been wrong, and he would be coming home today, and she was going to have to tell him so.

Except she didn't. He came in the door that day with dinner in a brown paper bag, grease-stained and smelling fantastic. He plunked it on the table with the pride of a caveman presenting a slain beast.

He found her sitting on the patio, slumped against the sliding glass door and covered in grime, and he asked her what was wrong. She told him she had lost the ring. He took in her tragic expression and red eyes, and before she could say anything else, he told her not to cry, that it was all right. He grabbed her hands and helped her to stand, bringing her inside to get cleaned up. He hugged her, grease and all, smelled her hair and told her that he'd missed her, and he told her he'd brought home cheap Chinese and a bottle of wine.

Emily had always been under the misguided impression that once you realized that the love you had is gone, that it may not have ever existed in the first place, you couldn't possibly have a hankering for sweet and sour spareribs. Somehow some innate decency would stop you from sitting in silence across from the man who adores you, ingesting a plate full of fried rice and chicken balls.

She was dead wrong. You *can* do it. You can even enjoy it, and you can appreciate being cared for when you've had a hard day, and you can feel justified that you deserve a meal after rolling under all of the beds in your house. You can talk about his day and never once mention your absolute change of heart and the ultimate necessity of a parting of the ways.

Then you can hoist yourself up from the table, waddle over to the couch and realize you live with someone who doesn't care if you unzip your fly in a decidedly unsexy "ate so much you nearly split your pants" kind of way.

You can lie there comfortably drinking beer and mocking the people on your reality show of choice and remember how funny your boyfriend is.

When he reaches for your leg, you can let him, and when he asks if you're ready for bed, you can tell him that you are.

It turns out you can take the truth that your relationship is over and shove it so far down, you can ride out one month in this pleasant company, then another. One day, when your eye spies something sparkling near the baseboard in the kitchen, you can pick it up and slip it on the third finger of your left hand.

But once you are sure that you have fallen out of love, you can't, and don't let anyone tell you differently, fall back.

Emily found this out on a very sunny Labour Day, when Stuart was actually labouring, sitting in a deserted office building trying to fix a bug in the most recent site he'd designed. She, for her part, had hoped to spend the day straightening up her, their, office. She hardly ever went in there except to Google the occasional restaurant or medical symptom, always tripping over boxes of paper and canvases and other miscellaneous crap Stuart had accumulated. Emily had always viewed September as the true beginning of the year, a hangover from school days, she supposed. It always brought about a fit of cleaning.

Hours passed as she made her way through his boxes of tax receipts and invoices, methodically sorting and filing and collecting an impressive pile for the shredder.

Next was Stuart's mess of a desk. Opening drawer after drawer, she plowed through until she opened the bottom drawer and saw something that made her stop sorting, even stop breathing for a moment.

It was a letter, sitting loosely atop a packet of other letters held together with one of her hair elastics, having been removed, presumably to be reread. They were letters she had written Stuart during a three-month period he'd been in Europe travelling with his mother. They'd been together just under a year at that time and had decided they'd stay together while he was gone. She picked up the page of loose leaf, feeling a bit like a thief, even though the words were hers. She started reading.

Dear Stuart,

Now what do I say? The first official letter. A LOVE letter at that. The pressure of it is crippling. But I will carry on because (gasp! Dare she say it?) I love you. I said it at the airport, and no, it wasn't just because you did. I said it because I do. So there. I miss you desperately,

*and I'm sitting here in a coffee shop like a graduate
student surrounded by people who have no relation to
me, and you are miles and miles across the ocean. How
can this be right? It's like time running backwards or
talking goats, completely unnatural. It's amazing the
things you can say in a letter, isn't it? Things you'd never
say to someone's face. All the things you can't say. The
Victorians were totally on to something.*

A drop hit the paper, telling Emily that she was
crying as she read this sheet full of her loopy writing
and sloppy sentiments. She hadn't known he had kept
these letters; she knew she hadn't kept his. She
continued reading.

*I can still see your face, though, if I screw my eyes
up tight. I thought for a second last night that I
couldn't, that you'd been pushed right out of my head
by the minutes from meetings and my desire to
remember to bring back the videos I rented. But you
are, in fact, still safely in view of my mind's eye... I just
checked. Can you see me? Have you looked? Go ahead
take a peek, I'll wait.*

She leaned back against the desk leg, wiping her eyes.
God, she sounded so young and sure of herself. So sweet
on him. She didn't feel any of that now. She read on.

*I'm sending this to Dublin. If you're reading it, I'm
assuming you have arrived safe and did not murder our
Glyniss on the trip over from Scotland. Is it raining in
Dublin? It's the odds-on favourite weather, I hear. It's cold*

and miserable here, I'm happy to report. It suits my mood. I could tell you that the angels are crying because we're apart, but I can't. And not just because it's too corny. It's not actually raining here at all. The sky is just grey and watery. No cherubic tears, angelic hay fever maybe. Hmmm, I guess that last bit wasn't very romantic, was it? I'll make it up to you. Just keep reading...

keep reading...

keep reading....

I'm not wearing panties. Hah! Said the girl who misses you more by the day.

Em

Emily folded the letter, unable to pick up the next one. Even as she looked into a drawer full of proof, she couldn't remember loving Stuart that way. Like her ring when it was missing, she could not remember its brilliance.

Whatever she felt for him now, it could never be that. And if she was ever to have a hope of feeling that way again, she was going to have to tell him so.

But how? How do you tell a man who saved your love letters that you wanted to break his heart? The answer was in her hands. The things you can't say, you write. That was why Stuart came home that evening to find a note waiting for him on the kitchen table.

There are only two kinds of letters that lovers send to one another, the love letter, and the Dear John. It is easy enough for even the most ineloquent writer to knock off a love letter. But the Dear John is another beast entirely.

A person should never have their heart broken that way. It's cruel and cowardly. But if you are going to end things in this unchivalrous fashion, the letter should always be handwritten. Emily's was.

It should not, however, be written on a lined yellow paper pad with a ballpoint pen, lest it be perceived from a distance as a shopping list. Which is, sadly, what happened to Stuart, leaving him quite unprepared for the shock of what he was about to read:

Stuart,

I want to tell you something. And I want to say it in a way that will make you understand how very much I have loved you. And why that has changed.

It's not going to be easy. I don't have a noble reason. I think you should know that.

You want to hear one, I guess. You want to hear that I don't think I'm worthy of you, or that I'm trying to protect you, or that I'd been walking along the street one day and found my one and only soulmate and had to be with him.

But I can't tell you any of those things.

You'll want me to convince you that I don't know it's going to break your heart that I've left, or that I'm only going for a little while to see if I may come back.

But I can't tell you any of those things either.

Maybe you'd even settle for me telling you that I've never really loved you, and it just took me three years to get around to telling you.

But I'm not sure that's true. I did love you at some point, and I may still, just not in the right way.

I guess this is the point where I say I'm leaving you, though I guess you'll be the one that's going, and I'm sorry for that too. That looks awful, what I just wrote.

Awful and true. I guess what I'm really saying is it's over. I'm sorry to be a coward and say it on paper, but I couldn't stand to see your face when you found out.
Love, (Again I'm sorry, it's awful and true)
Emily

She had thought it kinder to end that way, to seal the poisoned epistle with love. That was bullshit, he thought.

Stuart was reeling, literally. He was holding on to a chair so that he wouldn't fall over. He had just been gone a few hours. This couldn't have come to her today. She'd had this lined up, ready, maybe for days.

He sat trying to process what he'd read, tipping the large double double he'd brought in for himself into his mouth in long burning gulps. Then he drank the one he'd brought for her, as the questions flooded his brain. She wanted to leave him? He had to go? She didn't love him? She did?

He was devastated and confused. He had loved Emily for what seemed like forever. How could she leave him with all of these questions?

In fact, she hadn't. He heard her before he saw her. She was hovering by the kitchen door. She'd been waiting for him to come home and read it, and she'd been there the whole time.

He felt sick, and after a mad dash for the bathroom, he was. Re-scalding his esophagus with the coffee he'd just drunk. It burned. Everything burned. Then, not knowing what else to do, he cried his goddamned eyes out.

He was in there for almost an hour, during which

time Emily made a guilty walk across the kitchen to the bathroom door, running her nails softly up and down the wood grain, then asking if he couldn't let her in. Asking if he was okay.

He was *so* not okay.

He might be in there still, the sorrow seemed so great, if she hadn't then asked him not to do anything stupid, since her Ritalin pills were in the bathroom cupboard.

Kill himself? In the bathroom of their, her, fucking condo? With a bottle of Ritalin? He was so insulted that his indignation propelled him to his feet, out of the bathroom and through the front door.

It wasn't indignation that made him call her a "stupid cunt" before slamming the door behind him, and it wasn't the shock or the pain. He said it because as much as he loved her, and as much as he was going to miss her, Emily could be a really big cunt sometimes, and a stupid one too, the whole Ritalin-as-a-suicide device thing being a prime example, the letter being another. Who does that? Then waits around to see your reaction? You know who does that? A stupid cunt, that's who. And now, as she had so clearly made it known, he had nothing to lose by telling her so. So he had.

On that day in September, the first day of the year that she left, everything had changed, and nothing had changed.

The fact that he loved her hadn't changed. The fact that she didn't love him hadn't changed. Not that day anyway. He hadn't lost his soul, or his manhood, or his need to keep breathing.

Not the fact that the girl he'd loved for so many

years, and he did love her, was a bit controlling and a bit manipulative and had never thought that he could really make it as an artist. Or that she had always made fun of his mother and always been jealous of Elizabeth and never really tried to get close to her, even though Elizabeth was one of the few people in this world Stuart thought of as a friend.

Those were just the things that popped into his head unbidden on the ride down the elevator.

He loved her so much, his body was aching at the loss of her. But it did not make her perfect.

Still in shock, Stuart walked himself over to his local bar, a pub called appropriately enough, The Local, almost without thinking. He ordered a pint, hoping it would soothe his singed throat, and attempted to wrap his head around the fact that he was now heartbroken and homeless. Then he ordered another, because the first one had tasted good. Then another. Then he decided if he ordered a pitcher, he could cut his wait time between drinks. He sat there sipping and lost in thought, mulling things over until a heavy arm landed on his shoulder, and a slurred voice asked if "I can get a little of that."

Stuart's particular brand of misery did not demand company, especially from a greasy fat guy who'd probably been there all day, so he shrugged off the offending limb, trying to pretend he hadn't heard the man. This produced a low rumbling growl from the fatty, who turned to the bartender, saying he was none too impressed with the "fuckin' piece of shit too fuckin' cheap to share his fuckin' beer."

Stuart sighed and pushed what was left in the

pitcher down the bar before sliding off his stool and walking out the door. He didn't want to give it up. Didn't want to leave, having nowhere else to go. But he also didn't want to get himself in a fight, or as he liked to call them, beatings.

Stuart was a big guy, tall and not overly thin, but he was not a tough guy. Blame it on being raised by an overly doting mother, but he just did not have a killer instinct. He could not fight at the best of times and certainly did not have it in him that night. Standing up, he could barely keep his knees from giving out. This was not due to the fear of an impending ass kicking, nor due to the fact that he'd had more to drink than was usual even for him. No. On top of being dumped, on top of forcing him to seek solace in a bar where ugly men said ugly things, Emily had given him a cold. He'd felt it slowly settling over him while he'd been at work that day. It that had lit upon her lightly the weekend before but was destined to take him down to hell and back. Typical.

Out on the street, he felt lost. He hadn't been ready to face the world yet, and he had no idea how to go about it. Knowing he was not far from an area frequented by hookers, he had a wild notion that he should go find one. He could forget things for a while and have a place to lie down, but an increasing urge to vomit curbed the desire, and not only that—truth be told, Stuart had never actually attempted to pick up a hooker before. Not because he was in any way against it, but because of a fear that he might be rejected. And a fear of diseases.

He'd never told Emily about that. Never told anyone

but Elizabeth. She'd laughed when he'd told her and said it wasn't very rock and roll.

He wondered what things Emily had never told him, and it made him so tired, he sat right down on the pavement so he could have a rest.

From that vantage point, Stuart came to realize a few things. The first; that he was kind of drunk. The second; that he had given his heart to a woman, and while it was something that she made clear she didn't want, she hadn't been able to return it. It was still there, with her, beating quietly, unwanted, apologizing and trying not to cause offence. The third; he was, in fact, quite drunk and wouldn't be getting up off the ground any time soon.

He was uncomfortable sitting there on the pavement littered with cigarette butts and the dark spots left by people's gobs of spit. He was even more uncomfortable when he realized he was sitting across from the homeless guy he always meant to buy a coffee for but never had. He waved, got no response and felt like a dick for a minute before deciding it was better to feel sorry for himself than somebody else.

I'm going to end up just like him, Stuart thought, feeling cold and lonely and resentful of the sad looks happy people were shooting him on their way to more important things. They couldn't see a difference between the two men taking up real estate on the sidewalk. In his self-pitying stupor, neither could Stuart.

"I could just die here tonight," he mumbled to the twinkling stars, to Emily packing his things as he sat there, to himself. "I should just die."

"The only way you're going to die tonight is if I kick

your ass for leaving a woman sitting alone at the bar for the past hour," replied a voice somewhere overhead.

A woman's face appeared to him. For a moment Stuart let himself believe that she might be an angel. His guardian angel, come to take him home. Wherever that was now.

But when he felt her stick an icy hand under his head, propping him up roughly against a building, Stuart knew who she was. He knew she wasn't an angel, and he knew that she was pissed. He tried to tell her he was sorry he'd forgotten to meet her. He tried to tell her he had a cold, and he wanted to ask her if she could help him up, because the sidewalk was damp.

What he said was, "It was her condo, but it was MY ring, Liz, and she LOST it!"

Then Stuart started to cry.

"Aw, Jesus. She chucked you," Elizabeth said as she grabbed his arm. "I knew she sounded weird on the phone. Bitchier than usual." She watched in horror as he blew his nose on her scarf.

"Oh, fuck. You're a mess. Okay, let's get you home."

Stuart's eyes welled up again as he choked out "Home?" Elizabeth sighed. "Well, my home then."

"Can we go get a drink first?"

"Do you think you need one?" she asked him.

"Desperately," he said in a voice so sad, she could easily kill over it.

"Okay, honey, one more drink. If you pass out, I'll get to tell you all about my news without feeling like a total asshole." She grabbed his shoulders and pointed him in the direction of her car.

*   *   *

Kate did not feel well as she stared at the huge empty spaces that now filled her apartment, but she comforted herself with the knowledge that she had done the right thing.

She wished of course that it had worked out with Scott. It would have been so much easier just to be together. One more thing to cross off life's to-do list. Find a partner? Check.

She would have liked to have been able to hold on to the kind of man she could readily admit was a great catch. Considerate, employed, straight, good teeth. Even the last name was great. Archer. She would have been happy to be Katherine Archer. Katherine Mackenzie-Archer. Mrs. Archer, even.

But he seemed compelled to keep telling her stories that she'd heard before. A thousand times before. "One time in college, my buddies and I…" Took a road trip to B.C., chatted up a hot woman that ended up being a man, shaved a guy bald when he passed out on the couch.

She knew. She knew them all.

Then there was the way he was always grabbing the back of her neck when he drove, even though he knew she hated it when people touched her neck.

"I'm not grabbing it, I'm rubbing it," he'd say, like he was the one who'd been offended. "…and I'm not people. I'm your man."

Yes, that's right. He referred to himself as "her man". He did this all the time. In public. Alone it was worse, since he had the tendency to call himself "her big man".

Not only awful, but woefully overstated.

Well, maybe that was unfair. He was fine, definitely not porn star material or anything, but fine. That was not a problem. The problems were much smaller, but they were lethal.

He was a guy who picked her birthday cards out at the drug store, the most recent monstrosity still up for viewing on the entertainment unit. It had an elephant on it, a pink one. What newly thirty-year-old woman wouldn't be charmed to know her boyfriend looked across a sea of birthday cards, spied one with the biggest, ugliest animal in the world on the front, and said "Aha! Perfect!"?

He was a guy who took his socks off in the living room at the end of the day, then shoved them in his pocket.

And the socks...

Scott wore black ones that snaked up his leg to mid calf, where they were secured by the tightest band of elastic imaginable. It was amazing there was any blood left in his ankles. They were made out of some poly-rayon-plastic blend. Kate could see them glisten when they caught the light. They shone like asphalt on a sunny day. At times, she'd been tempted to scream, "What did cotton ever do to you?" but he would have laughed about it. Scott laughed about everything.

He had no passion in him. Even as Kate had sat him down to tell him it was over, he'd just looked at her with a stupid smile on his face. It had stayed, even as she'd told him how miserable she was. How she'd rather be alone than be with him.

When she finished, she dissolved in a puddle of

tears. No, not dissolved. Kate wasn't a graceful crier. She didn't have much practice at it, and she hated to cry. When she finished, she was red-eyed and snotty, jerking sporadically in her seat. He was still smiling, looking every bit like an indulgent parent.

He told her if she couldn't be happy with him, she'd better do her best to be happy some other way, because that's all he wanted for her. It was very wise and very kind, and while it should have made her feel like shit, all it did was mildly irritate her, because he'd said it in what she liked to call his "Obi Wan" voice.

Oh. He was a Star Wars fanatic too, even the new crappy ones.

So the whole time he was wishing her well, Kate found she'd become fixated on the wet spot his beer bottle was leaving on the coffee table. *Her* coffee table.

Scott couldn't keep his beer in the fridge like normal people. He had to stockpile his beer in the freezer. Nice and frosty and dripping like hell, even the coasters couldn't control it. When he remembered to use a coaster. Both times.

Kate couldn't count the number of guests who'd had to take their beer with a spoon. It was so embarrassing. Or the number of times he'd forgotten they were in there, and they'd exploded all over the ManMeal frozen dinners he insisted on buying.

These were the things popping into her head as Scott offered up the best graduation speech ever. He hit all the key points; follow your path, spread your wings, if you love someone, set them free.

Even as she stood drowning in the nothingness, once stockpiled with electronic equipment and Storm

Trooper figurines, Kate knew this decision had been the right one. It wasn't a regret that made her feel ill. Her problem was, now that she'd made the big hard decision, how in the world was she going to make the next one?

Things had happened so quickly since they'd ended things. A talk on Friday night, another on Saturday morning, during which Scott had enquired whether the night he'd spent in the office/spare room had changed her mind. When she said it hadn't, it took just three short car trips for him to remove all that was his from the apartment they were sharing. He'd graciously suggested that she should keep the apartment, since it was close to the subway line, and she had no car.

In the whirl, she had managed to avoid having to think beyond the break-up. But on this holiday Monday, with everything neatly and more or less equitably divided (she'd let him have the coffee table), she had nothing but time to think.

What was she supposed to do now that she was back on the market? *Was* she back on the market? How long was she supposed to stay in mourning? One month, three months. Oh God, was she going to be alone at Christmas?

Would it be bitchy to go out on the town? Was it all her fault? Which friends should she tell first? The whole thing had her thrown. She'd never broken up with someone before. How upset was she expected, entitled, to be here? At the moment, all she felt was a mild ache in her temple and a sense of relief.

The phone rang, and Megan's number popped up on the call display. It sounded like salvation. Megan would know what to do. Megan would understand. She was Kate's smart friend, the lawyer.

"You'd better be calling with a plan and a pocket full of money," Kate said in lieu of hello, sounding almost giddy.

"What? Honey, how are you? Are you drunk?"

"No, I'm not drunk. But I'm single."

"Holy shit. You did it? How *are* you?"

"I'm not very sorry that he left, and I'm not super-glad he's gone, and I think I would like to be drunk. Oh, and how are you?"

"Not nearly as conflicted," said Megan. "I'm on my way over, I guess, but the liquor store is closed today, so I'll have to make a stop at my parents' to raid the liquor cabinet, and I'll have to stay for a coffee. I'll be at least an hour. Are you okay till then?"

"Yeah. I think there's still some frozen beer here to keep me company."

"Lovely. Should we call your sister?"

Kate didn't even have to think about it. "Hell, no. Not yet. I want people who are going to be nice to me this evening; people who actually liked me more than they liked Scottie. I'm guessing that boils down to about you."

"Oh, Katie…hang in. I'll be there soon."

"I did the right thing here, huh, Meg?"

"I have no idea."

"I didn't love him."

"Well then, at least you did him a favour."

"I guess."

"So what am I bringing over?"

"Wine. Red. A big bottle, if they've got it."

"Jesus, Kate, I know that. What do think I am, an amateur?" Meg said. "But merlot, shiraz, what do you want."

"Merlot."

"'kay, I'll be there soon."

Kate listened as Megan hung up, keeping the phone to her ear until she heard the dial tone. Setting the receiver in its cradle, she realized she'd just made her first post-break-up decision, and it hadn't been so hard. Smiling, she wandered into the kitchen, opening the drawer next to the sink to pull out a spoon before setting her sights on the freezer.

October

There are at least half a dozen very good rock songs that offer convincing arguments that it is better to go down swinging than to be simply swept away, but at this hour of the morning, Kate was hard pressed to remember any of them. At this time of day, it seemed inconceivable that she could muster up the effort necessary to defend herself from this verbal onslaught.

It was much easier just to wait it out, glassy-eyed, and take it.

So she sat silently as she was fired. Again. Ending her stint at the fourth accountancy firm she'd been dismissed from this year.

The first time she'd been tearful, the second put out. By round three, a sense of déjà vu had left her feeling only mild amusement. Now, staring down the barrel of number four, her general attitude could be best described as resigned.

Until this one, Kate had told herself that it was the slow-growing cancer of her relationship with Scott that had made her so unhappy at work, that had made her barely competent. But now she realized she just didn't like accounting.

In all cases, she'd have been happy to scream "I

quit!" but had remained silent until her total lack of enthusiasm and work ethic said it for her. This time was no different.

With her newly old boss still leaning over his desk, one pudgy, accusatory finger still wagging, the saliva still glistening at the corners of his mouth, she stood, exited the room, grabbed her purse and ficus plant from the desk and saw herself out.

It was just after nine o'clock in the morning, and her time was once again her own. It didn't feel too bad. It was sort of like sliding on shoes you haven't worn in a while. Perhaps a little uncomfortable, but so familiar in a way, you don't mind it.

After the events of last month, she hardly noticed. The break-up hadn't been too traumatic, quite civilized really. But the adjustment to a life on her own had left her exhausted. His leaving in the abstract had seemed cut and dry. The problem had been that they were two separate people, whole entities that would simply head off in two different directions.

It was while clearing out the apartment that she began to realize this was untrue. It seemed there was a bit of both of them in every object in the place. There were many things he'd brought into her life that she'd never thought she'd have to part with, never thought she'd have to miss. Not the big things, the TV or the stereo. It was when he'd come back the week after he moved out to pick up his magazine rack that she'd felt her heart sink. She didn't even like it, but it had been there. It had been theirs. She hadn't known that she could cry over something like that.

His old high-school hockey jersey had been another

example. She'd slept in it off and on in the weeks after he'd left. He saw it on the top of a hamper of clean laundry set out to be folded and grabbed for it without even asking. She bit her tongue in her effort not to ask his permission to keep it. That's not just a figure of speech. People really do it. Sometimes they'll even bite right through, trying so hard to stop themselves from being found out for who they are, when they are trying to do what's right, or what's expected. She had ended this, and she was in no position to be sentimental or selfish or angry or sad. All she could be was dry-eyed and apologetic. She didn't protest one thing that he packed in the boxes. There weren't so many; he wasn't trying to ruin her. He was taking only the things he'd need to set up his own place, the things she'd always said she didn't care for, and he was being wonderful about it.

The worst, though, was that he took all of the pictures they'd had in the place, photos of the two of them together. He didn't ask, because he didn't think he needed to. When she grabbed the last one sitting out in the living room, he was genuinely surprised, saying that he hadn't thought she'd want them and didn't want to think of them being thrown out in the trash. She tasted blood as she placed it on the top of the box he was holding. As she pushed the door for his final exit, she was impressed at his timing, waiting until this moment to break her heart as well.

Once it was over, Kate had then faced the utter nightmare of telling her parents and her older sister Tracy what she'd done. And now she'd have to add getting sacked to the list of disappointments.

Her family loved Scott, possibly more than they loved Kate. They would call to speak to him, even when she wasn't there, to check up on him and fill him in on their lives. Keep him in the family loop. He always pretended he didn't mind, and they loved him for it. He always returned their calls. He was a better daughter than she was, and bringing him into the fold had been her greatest familial achievement.

There had been some explaining to do and blame to accept and tears to count as they rolled down her mother's face. Her mother wasn't a pretty crier either.

In comparison to that, the fact that her services were no longer needed at Anderson-Smith and Co. didn't bother her in the least. It was not only accounting that she didn't care for, but accountants too. She had never taken delight in correcting people's faulty sums in public meetings or whipping out a solar-powered key chain calculator at restaurants. In fact, she was pretty sure she was done with the field altogether. It hadn't been her choice in the first place. Her father had steered her towards it after seeing she had a knack for numbers and little interest in anything at all.

That she was broke didn't bother her either. In fact, in her mind, Kate wasn't broke…yet. She had some outstanding salary to collect, some vacation pay coming to her and a tiny amount saved in a house fund. She was going to be broke, no doubt, and soon. But not today.

Today she could still take herself over to the fancy coffee shop, where they sprinkled cinnamon on absolutely everything, to buy a little treat to cheer herself up. She was rather fond of cinnamon.

She sat at a window table, with her plant at her feet and her hands wrapped around an enormous steaming cup, and felt satisfied. Changing her relationship status had not changed her life. She had thought it might. She was busting to *be* something, somebody new and/or improved. But she was still waking up in a beige-walled bedroom, albeit alone, and walking over to her beige-walled office and sitting in her beige-walled cubicle to count the seconds that make up an eight-hour day, all 28,800 of them. But this, this was a change. Whatever she might be and never be, she was no longer an accountant in the employ of Anderson-Smith. She was sitting in a coffee shop in the middle of the morning with all of the other people who don't go to work from nine to five. People who live a different life. It was a step in the right direction, even if it was not one she'd made proactively. Staring at the people walking down the street in no apparent hurry, she was happy.

For about ten minutes. Then she saw a woman walking down the street who seemed in a very big hurry indeed. Someone familiar, and Kate realized that she had a big "I told you so" coming to her.

It was likely she had more than one. She had become quite the spectacular failure in the work department, but there was one to come from a most unpleasant source. A screeching, gloating, judgmental source who had just seen Kate and her plant sitting in the café window.

She took a long, slow sip of her coffee and tried to savour it on a level that would carry her through what was about to happen. Opening her eyes, she saw her sister still there, standing in the window, waiting to be acknowledged. Kate smiled and gave a little wave. Tracy gestured towards the plant with her thumb, and Kate just gave a little shrug, watching her sister turn back towards the café entrance.

Tracy knew. It wasn't the ficus's fault, the plant had simply been confirmation. No, she'd known it the minute she'd looked over and seen Kate sitting there. There were no secrets from Tracy, or Hawk-Eye, as their father had dubbed her. The girl had an uncanny knack for sizing you up in a heartbeat and an evil habit of broadcasting your innermost secrets in stereo. Kate remembered:

Walking out of the bathroom one day shortly after her twelfth birthday; "OH MY GOD! You've got your PERIOD!"

At sixteen, running up the stairs, brown bag in hand; "OH MY GOD! You're on the PILL!"

At twenty-three, sitting down to dinner, dry-eyed and tight-lipped: "OH MY GOD! He DUMPED YOU!"

Thinking about it, she couldn't recall any event in her life that hadn't been conveyed to her family in this way. Older and wiser, Tracy had been the narrator of Kate's life for over a quarter century.

Not that Kate wouldn't have liked to get a word in edgewise every once in a while, to set some things straight. It is the privilege of family to know every single thing and understand absolutely nothing. But trying to stop Tracy was as productive as trying to slow down a freight train by blowing on it.

No, Kate had learned, it was so much easier to just sit there glassy-eyed and take it. Being Tracy's little sister was the only job she'd never managed not to lose, and as much as it pained her to admit it, she wouldn't quit this one either.

Draining the last of her cup even as her bladder protested, she ran her finger around the inside rim, collecting the last of the sweetness as her sister's shoes clacked closer to her table.

Kate sucked the finger clean and sat up straight. She was ready now. "Hi, Trace."

"OH MY GOD! They SACKED you!"

* * *

Mini sandwiches. Jesus. A culinary dropkick to the spirit of post-menopausal woman everywhere. The grey hairs, the nannies, the tea cozy and house slipper set.

A food reflective of the women they are made by and for. Fragile, bland antiquities trotted out for praise at celebrations and funerals.

Considered the height of elegance to those who wouldn't know elegance if it came up and bit them in the ass, if you asked Glyniss.

She turned her eyes from the tiered silver tray laden with sandwiches never classified as tasty, but dainty. And who the hell would want to eat dainty food? Who wants to ensure their survival through the consumption of the sickening combination of eggs and mayonnaise served up on a plate in miniature Swiss rolls? Or via pimento and asparagus spears stuck at a jaunty angle from duck liver pâté sitting on a cracker?

"Who eats these things?" she asked her luncheon companions.

"Women of a certain age, dear," replied the woman to

her left, a tiny, straight-backed, proper sort of woman. All silver hair and pearls. The kind of lady who removes her coins from a change purse that closes with a crisp and satisfying snap. "And like it or not, that means you."

Glyniss did not like it at all. She had hoped that having successfully (more or less) raised her sons and left her job behind, she would be afforded the blessing of quickly shedding her mortal coil, never to be burdened with the grey pubic hair, creaking joints or moderate incontinence a long life would ensure.

She was quite tiny herself. Glyniss had never bothered the world by taking up too much space with her presence. She doubted it would even notice if she up and disappeared. But if her last physical results were to be believed, her farewell was going to be a slow fade. Healthy as a horse, her doctor had informed her, only to top that unwelcome comparison by predicting that "It's your mind that will go before that heart of yours gives out. Ha Ha."

More's the pity.

Of course, that wasn't the sort of thing you said to Aunt Agathe, the family matriarch and sergeant major, who was for all intents and purposes the mother Glyniss never had.

To clarify, Glyniss did have a mother. A flighty, jealous and beautiful creature who could never decide which was worse, that her daughters should turn out not to be beautiful, or that they would.

Glyniss's DNA, it seemed, had chosen the option less likely to end in the consumption of a poisoned apple, and assembled itself in a plain and pale formation. A clumsy, shy one at that.

So she was starved and taunted and threatened until she was abandoned altogether, leaving Aunt Agathe to instruct and encourage and make sure Glyniss's life was not only sustained, but amounted to something.

It was also not the sort of thing she would ever say in front of her sister, Helen.

Helen had decided to emerge from the birth canal much like Athena through Zeus's skull. A fully formed Amazon, Helen had hit the earth blonde and beautiful, somehow armored and immune to their mother's jealousies and neglectfulness. Helen hadn't cried when she'd woke one morning to find their mother had left, or when the letter had arrived saying she had died in a car accident halfway around the world a few years later. And she'd never spoken of her since.

Unlike Glyniss, Helen had fought for her senior years with a vengeance. Losing a breast in the battle, she had emerged victorious and more than willing to embrace all that golden age had to offer. Senior moments and senior discounts, afternoon teas, extra fibre cereals, as well as the God-given right to say whatever the hell she felt like saying and to keep a watchful and reproachful eye on her neighbours' comings and goings.

The yellow teeth, falling uterus, grandchildren and saggy boobs, well boob, Helen thought it was all pretty hilarious. And Glyniss, with her A+ medical record, was too ashamed to disagree.

Which is why she was sitting on a hard plywood chair with her stocking catching on the mechanics of a folding card table draped in a lace cloth, as she meekly granted her aunt's request that she pass the cream and sugar.

They were seated among a sea of other women in the slightly dank and heavily linoleumed parish hall of Agathe's church.

The sisters, Helen and Glyniss, had been summoned early in the week. They were there, supposedly, to raise money for new hymnals which would provide the female congregation the necessary means to practice the other pastime deemed suitable for them, singing in the church choir.

But that was not why they were really there. They were there to talk to Glyniss about Stuart. They were concerned.

In the wee morning hours of the day after Labour Day, Stuart had arrived at his mother's apartment building, drunk, broke and without the means to pay the cab driver who had brought him there.

He'd left Elizabeth alone to wait on yet another pitcher of beer and headed for the bathroom. Coming out, he had felt the overwhelming urge to flee. Standing at the urinal, holding on to the wall for support, it had come to him that there was still one place in the world that he could still technically call home. By the time he'd finished and zipped his fly, it was clear to him that he wanted his mother. With the idea planted, he couldn't get himself there fast enough. He forgot to wash his hands, forgot Elizabeth's kind offer to stay at her place...forgot Elizabeth entirely, along with the bar tab. *His* tab, since Elizabeth had her car and had been reduced to drinking tap water. He stumbled out the door and into a taxi. From there it was a twenty minute and thirty-five dollar trip to Glyniss's door.

When Stuart stepped out of the cab, he realized he

did not have thirty-five dollars, or ten dollars or two. So he began to ring the door buzzers of a random selection of his mother's neighbours, calling "Sanctuary, sanctuary" into the intercom.

The driver, desirous of his fare and a quick escape from his obviously obliterated, possibly deranged passenger, managed to tease the right call number from Stuart's muddled mind, waking Glyniss from what had been a fitful and unsatisfying sleep.

Picking up the phone to hear an accented description of a son downstairs in a bad way with no money to pay for his cab ride, she immediately brought to mind an image of her younger son Graham. But even as she could see his hazel eyes staring back at her, she could hear it was the voice of her older boy coming through the static.

"Sanctuary!"

She threw on slippers and donned a robe. Leaving the curlers in her hair, she stopped only to put on a splash of lipstick before grabbing her purse and heading for the lobby. She wasn't about to buzz in a stranger; especially one who was audibly so unlike herself.

She said "stranger" even in her own head, but she knew what she really meant. Foreigner. And she knew it was wrong to mean it. But that didn't change a thing.

Two unkind assumptions in about as many minutes, she noted. She knew it was wrong always to think the worst of Graham. She knew it was wrong not to buzz in foreigners. She was a bad mother and a bit of a racist. She knew it, and she could live with it.

The elevator stopped, and the doors slid open, offering Glyniss a view of her baby staring at her through the glass. He waved.

He looked half-cocked, and just like his father. She bristled but decided she wouldn't mention that, even if it meant biting through her tongue. She was going to get this right.

She took a breath and opened the main door, wider than necessary to try to give the impression that she had no fear of this brown-skinned man who was holding her son ransom.

She pulled Stuart through the doors, handing the man two crisp twenties from her purse and thanking him profusely for bringing her son home. She sympathized that it must be terrible work having to bring home people like this, especially when in his old country he must have been "a doctor or scientist or something." She told him she'd seen those commercials and thought the whole immigration process was such a crying shame.

Then she wished him a pleasant night and turned toward the elevator, resisting the urge to push the automatic door shut. Instead, she walked slowly, followed by Stuart, but stopping to open her purse and conduct a pretend key search until she heard the door click shut. It was all very well and good to be polite, but she wasn't about to grant some stranger free access to the building.

Satisfied, she brought her boy up to her apartment, settling him on the couch before asking him what this was all about.

He hiccupped, then giggled, finally sighing as he said, "Emily broke up with me, but she still loves me, I think, but it's over I think, so I don't live there any more, and I had to come home. Can I get a glass of water or something? I am totally dry."

Artfully ignoring the word "had", Glyniss focused almost gleefully on the word "home". Her boy wanted home. All motherly insecurities were momentarily swept away by the fact that in this time of crisis, her son had chosen her. She was a good mother. She was not *her* mother. Stuart had just proved it.

Stuart had never let her down.

Glyniss was saddened, of course, that he had been tossed aside. Well, not saddened really. Piqued. She'd never liked that Emily anyway. She was a bit on the vulgar side and was always chasing some cause or another. She had cost Glyniss a small fortune in donations to save baby seals and to stop bio-farming. But she had never once got her socially conscious behind out of her seat to help clean up the dinner dishes. Glyniss was sorry to see Stuart looking so terrible over the whole thing. Still, she couldn't help feeling good about feeling needed.

Stuart wanted some water, and the responsibility was hers. She ran to the kitchen to fill up a glass, searching her cupboards for something he could put in his stomach to save him some agony in the morning.

Hugh, his father, had always fancied something salty when he'd rolled in from a night on the town. But it had been years since she'd kept the kinds of nuts and pretzels he preferred on hand. In the end, she grabbed a box of soda crackers and headed back to Stuart.

He thanked her for the water, and when she sat beside him and started to stroke his hair, he let her. Even though she felt him tense, he didn't pull away.

Victory. They sat there until his glass was empty. Until Stuart placed it on the ground, and, tipping to the left, landed his head on the arm of the sofa.

He'd been there ever since. That was six weeks ago. Glyniss had become, voluntarily, a slave to his every whim. It had been an honour, then a duty, and was now, frankly, a large, boring drain. She had mentioned this to her sister the last time they'd spoken on the phone. She had asked for sympathy but had also expected praise. "You're a good mother, Glyniss. There's a good girl."

It had been a mistake. Helen thought her less a saint than a sucker and had hung up after telling her so, only to pick it up again to call Agathe.

Naturally, Glyniss's presence had been requested. She was to be called on the carpet to explain, to defend why she would spend her days fetching a grown man's bathrobe and favourite cereal and preferred magazines, because he refused to get his lazy ass off the couch.

There wasn't even any small talk to prepare her before the questioning began.

"Did Stuart drop you off?" Agathe asked, innocent as a vulture.

"Well, no, Stuart doesn't have a car."

"I thought he had a flashy car."

"That's Graham, Aunt Aggie"

"Oh, yes. Graham does have the nice car. Did he walk you over then?"

"No, I was running late and hopped in a cab."

"I see."

They smiled at each other and stirred their tea. Helen shifted her chair a bit to fill the silence.

"What's he going to be up to today?" the older woman continued, circling.

"Oh. I'm not sure," Glyniss replied brightly. Too brightly. Her cheeks began to burn.

"Really. If I've heard correctly, I believe he'll be sitting in your living room concocting shopping lists of ridiculous items for you to fetch for him upon your return." The first grenade had been lobbed.

"I can't imagine where you heard that," Glynnis said, glaring at Helen, only to find that Helen wasn't looking even the slightest bit sheepish.

"Oh, come off it, Glyn. You wouldn't have been complaining about it if you hadn't had enough of it," Helen said calmly. "And we know you can't ever stand up for yourself, so you want us to stand up for you. That's why you called. Admit it."

Glyniss felt her body slump. She was deflated. Not because Helen was right, but because she was always so wrong. She didn't want Stuart to go, and she didn't want them to tell her that she did. She wanted to tell them that it was hard, and he was sad, and he never said thank you for any of it. She wanted *them* to say thank you, and she wanted to know that what she was doing was deserving of thanks.

She said none of this, of course. No one ever did. "Stuart is going through a horrible time right now, and he needs a little sympathy and support."

Helen waved the explanation away with her spoon, saying firmly, and quite coldly to Glyniss's ears, "I know he broke up with Emily, and that they dated a long time, and it must be hard, but he did not lose a limb. He's not disabled, he's disinclined. There is a huge difference."

"And either way, darling, it's not you who should be punished for this woman's betrayal," added Agathe. "Don't let the boy treat you poorly. You've done too much for him to ever allow that." She had that air of authority that made it nearly impossible for Glyniss to ever argue with her.

But she would argue today. For Stuart and for herself, she would put up a fight.

"He's not mistreating me," she started, remembering as soon as she said it that she'd armed her sister with a litany of complaints, proving that, in fact, he was. She went on hurriedly. "Not on purpose. He's a sensitive boy, and he needs my understanding."

"He's not sensitive, he's spoiled, and he feels sorry for himself, and he feels entitled to take it out on you because you've always let him," Helen said, condemning both mother and son in the same staid, matter-of-fact tone one uses to tell the time.

"How dare you," Glynnis said hotly. She could taste the tears before she felt them, thick in her throat.

"Now, girls," Agathe interjected. "We are not here, Helen, to burden your sister further. Glyniss, we know that Stuart has always been special to you. We are simply worried you are letting that cloud your reaction to his current predicament in a way that may be harmful to you both."

The attempt at diplomacy was lost in what Glyniss heard as a veiled accusation, made worse because it was true.

"So I'm a doormat, and I pick favourites? What's coming next? That I picked a drunk for a husband, and my divorce tainted the family? That I didn't save enough

money to retire like you wanted? Going to remind
everyone that I used to steal the penny candy, Helen? I'm
such a mess, it's a wonder you can stomach to look at me."

Glyniss had said this in an attempt to be cool and
cutting. But she could not control the wobble in her
voice and had managed to jostle a good quantity of the
tea from her cup with a waving hand.

"Everyone is looking at you, dear," said Agathe
through a tight smile. She would not be the object of
her Ladies Circle gossip.

Helen, infuriatingly, remained unfazed by the
outbursts, looking neither sorry, nor angry, but smiling
as she said, "Glyn, I've got no problem with you having
a favourite. Everyone has a favourite. I personally think
my son's an idiot and can't believe he's mine by blood. I
just think it's odd that your favourite's Stuart. I never
did understand that."

To some it would be hard to understand, since
Graham, Glynnis's younger boy, was the one with his
life together. The wife, the job, the car, the confidence.
It was Graham who had carried them through the first
few months after Hugh's leaving, when Stuart hardly
left his room and Glyniss couldn't quite get herself
motivated to pay the bills or buy the groceries. He was
the one who never asked for anything.

Graham was the baby. In a way, he was the reason
she and Hugh had split up, much in the same way that
Stuart's surprise appearance was the reason they had
gotten together.

Glyniss and Hugh had been dating only briefly
when she became pregnant. They had not been in love,
but they had been intimate. That was enough of a

reason for Hugh to propose, once Agathe had shown up at his boarding house one day and left five thousand dollars poorer.

Glyniss had been thrilled by his interest, the subsequent stroking and thrusting, and finally, his offer to make a legitimate woman of her. The day he proposed, she felt like she had dodged a bullet. Not that of family scandal, but of spinsterhood, which would have been worse. Glyniss was thirty-two years old at the time.

She had wanted to be a bride and a wife, and she was, all because of Stuart. In the few short months that it took the new couple to invest Agathe's "wedding present" in a decent bungalow and set up house, Glyniss had managed to turn a blind eye to Hugh's late nights and red eyes and stumbles over the steps upstairs.

Just when it seemed that things would settle and she would have to face the nights alone with no boxes to unpack or curtains to hang, Stuart had arrived, all sweet smells and chub. His big blue eyes staring into hers, he looked to her for everything, wanting her always near.

She was more than happy to spend her evenings by his cribside. Knowing in her heart that she had somehow pulled a fast one on Hugh with this marriage and baby business, she never requested that he spend time with his son or herself unless there was company present. He had done enough for her, and she was grateful.

Grateful enough to make his meals, clean up his messes and ignore his drunken ramblings. And, on occasion, to allow his drunken hands upon her, though he tended to find that comfort outside of their marriage bed, which suited them both.

Even as a youngster, Stuart had sensed this arrangement, staying far from his father unless he was called before him to sing a song or be taught to make fart noises or be tossed in the air and laugh, even though it frightened him. He was his mother's joy and his father's responsibility, and he knew he ought to be sorry for it.

In this way, they were not a dysfunctional family. They functioned quite well. And if they weren't a happy one, they were close enough for Glyniss and, it seemed, for Hugh.

Graham's arrival a few years later changed things. He was a handsome baby, as was Stuart, but he was not a pleasant one. He was quiet and solemn. He was so stone-faced, in fact, that his father had wondered if there wasn't something wrong with him. He slept through the night almost immediately and cried only for meals and when he was in need of a change. And, as a final insult, he only wanted those tasks performed by his father.

He didn't like being held by Glyniss. He didn't want to feed from her breast. He preferred to sit alone in a baby seat in the corner, unfussed until his father got home. Then he would cry, inconsolable, until he had his father's attention, until he had been seen.

But as he grew, he didn't want even that. He didn't much care for reciting the alphabet for a drunken audience or standing at the ready to play the role of loving son. He didn't like being fussed over by his mother. In fact, the only person who seemed to be able to do anything with him at all was Stuart.

Graham, it seemed, had the unfortunate talent, some might say the curse, of seeing things not as he'd like them to be, but as they really were. He knew that what was in his father's mug was not coffee. He knew that his mother knew too. He knew that his father did not like his children, and when he got old enough, he told his mother so. She had slapped him once, hard, thinking it would make him cry, but he simply put his hand to his cheek and walked away with his suspicions confirmed. Soon after, he also grew to know that his father was staying away for greater stretches at a time and that he would not be their father much longer. He knew that his mother thought it was his fault. He knew that when she told him that she wished he'd been born "more like his brother," she meant she wished he had not been born at all. When he was seven, he'd told her that, too. She'd slapped him again, for the last time.

She had been shocked to hear him say it and to know that it was true. Shocked to know that he was right. Her marriage was ending, and it was Graham's fault.

He wasn't a pleaser, this solemn boy. He knew that he was the cause of much unhappiness, but he did nothing to try to make them forget, to make up for it. He didn't play along in this game that they'd so carefully orchestrated. He didn't think he owed them for the trouble his presence had brought them.

It had taken the wind out of her, this moment of truth. But it had not knocked her down. It was something to file away in the deep, dark place we all pretend we don't have, and she'd gone to find Graham sitting on his bed holding his cheek, and she'd sat beside him and hugged him tight and told him she could not believe he would think such a thing, and she'd held on, though he struggled to get away from her for a very, very long time.

That night she had made her family an elaborate dinner featuring some of what she believed were Graham's favourite things, though he'd never stated a preference, so she couldn't be sure. Then she had cleaned up the dishes and tucked him into bed reading him what she thought to be his favourite story, even though he told her he was tired and turned away from her when she sat on the bed. Once she finished the book, she made herself a cup of tea and sat with it at the table watching a salty drop hit the formica, then another. That was when Stuart had come up behind her, putting a hand upon her shoulder.

"Are you crying, Ma?"

"No. Honey, I'm just a little tired from making dinner," she said, wiping her eyes and smiling at him.

"I'm sorry I didn't help you with the dishes, Ma," he said softly.

Glyniss looked at her sister and Aunt across the card table and thirty-odd years and said, "I don't have favourites. But Stuart is special, and he needs me, and what I don't need is a lecture."

"What you need is a good slap up the side of the head, and so does your boy there," said Helen, draining her cup.

"Helen, you are not helping Glyniss. And Glyniss, you are not helping Stuart. He needs to get his life going again, and if you are not the person to do it, then I know who is."

"You?" said Glyniss hopefully.

"I think she means your other favourite sissy," said Helen with a smirk.

"Helen! But yes, Glyniss, I think it's time you had Graham stop by for a chat."

November

In the weeks following the break-up, Stuart did little. He was frozen, paralyzed, but not for the reasons you'd think. Not the ones he'd thought, at least. He had always had the impression that if Emily ever left him he'd be ruined, he'd kill himself, since all life would stop for him anyway, wouldn't it?

He'd been floored by her leaving him. That's what he'd settled on calling it, although he'd been the one who had left. He'd been knocked down by the leaving, surely, but not out.

The morning after, he'd wanted to die, but that had more to do with the incredible hangover and the tongue-lashing he'd woken to when an irate Elizabeth, whose sympathy for him had vanished when she was forced to hand over forty dollars to pay a bar bill when she "wasn't even friggin' drinking, because I brought my friggin' car." That was before he'd asked his mother to screen his calls.

He didn't like being without Em, of course. He did love her. The way she smelled and the way she came to his gallery openings when they were held in coffee shops and no one else showed. How she ironed the towels that no one but the two of them saw. He wished they were still together, that the whole break-up had never happened, but to be honest, he didn't want her back. Not now. Every time he'd picked up the phone that day, he'd been forced to admit that you can't go back to a woman who would end a four-year relationship by writing you a letter; who would then hide in the shadows and watch you read it. How could you even think of going back to a girl like that?

Without the pining, and with the absolute certainty that they were less broken up than entirely dissolved, he was focusing his attention on the fact that his life was going to have three chapters. Before Emily, Emily, and now, After Emily. This was Stuart's problem.

A fairly even mix of romantic and doomsday prophet, once he and Emily had decided to form a unit, he'd naturally assumed that there was no alternative to it. It was them together or the end of the world. He believed in love. That it was that strong, that it could move mountains and work miracles and slay humble men where they stood. Why he believed this, considering the family in which he'd grown up, was a question he'd often been asked. The only answer he'd ever been able to offer in response was: he didn't know why, he just did.

He had loved Emily, truly and with all his heart. She was his one Big Love. He had waited for her his whole life. That was why, in the wake of loss, he had expected to feel utterly miserable. He had not been prepared to feel hungry sometimes, and bored sometimes, sitting there in the dark. Or that he'd remember to tune in for the new episode of his favourite medical drama.

He certainly hadn't expected to get an erection one

evening while sitting on his mother's couch watching a comely young singer on TV belting out a tepid rendition of some godawful pop sensation's latest hit. Not the week after his life was supposed to have ended. All of this mundane reality, this normalcy, this survival, what the hell was that about?

This was supposed to be a time of glorious despair. Dirty, dank, liquor-fuelled Nick Cave-esque despair.

He'd tried to do his part. He'd been drinking to excess. In fact, the only time he'd left the apartment was to take a trip to the LCBO when he realized he couldn't possibly live up to this ideal by drinking his mother's assortment of candy-flavoured liquors: Crème de Menthe and Cranberry Cooler, and to his horror, a bottle of Sex on the Beach, a gag gift from Aunt Helen.

He'd gone and bought some bottles of gin, as many as his bank balance could carry. He'd wanted to pick up the tough stuff, a J.D. or Wild Turkey, something harsh and self-damaging, but he knew he didn't have the stomach for it. One more indignity in this, his time of crisis.

So he'd been drinking and sitting and attempting to fall into stupor. But there was his mother to contend with, and her constant cleaning of the house and provision of fresh pajamas she'd picked up for him at The Bay, and the gifts of his favourite foods and magazines.

As much as he thought he should ride this out low and lonely, he liked the flannel bottoms and the smell of his crisp cotton pillowcase, and he did want "just a little nibble of brie" and the November issue of *Spin* magazine.

He realized that even though he woke each day with

a physical pain in his head and an imaginary one somewhere in the middle of his chest, the world was not only continuing, but he was interested in it.

And he was afraid of it. How was he going to insert himself into a world he never thought he'd have to deign to look at again? One where he would have to find his own home, manage his own money and make his own plans, alone. If he didn't have love in his life, what would he have?

That was what held him frozen. Not heartbreak, but fear; fear, then habit. He watched himself become a shining example of the law that a body at rest tends to stay at rest. He saw his mother's looks turn from concern to pity to tedium at his presence. He told himself every day that the next morning he'd stand up and shave and go grab a coffee in the morning, bring her back one too.

He made plans, lists. Stuart loved lists. He filled an entire notepad he'd pulled from his mother's bill-paying desk, first with things he loved about Emily, then things he hated. Then things he wanted to accomplish in life. These lists were supposed to calm him and make him feel in charge. Motivated people make lists. But even as he wrote them, he knew he couldn't fulfill them. He'd feel his pulse rise as the list got longer, one task, two tasks, three…too many. Even writing something as simple as a grocery list could make his heart pound in his ears. What did he want to eat? What of all the possible choices did he want for himself for dinner? What did he want?

So he started writing other lists, nonsense lists, like the list of words so pleasing to the ear, it's a wonder

that you don't hear them more often:
Demitasse
Melodious
Conundrum
Auspicious
Spectacular
Cantankerous
Extraordinary
Felicity
Doldrums
Forgiven
He was busting to get out and incapable of moving.
He was frozen. He was a mess, and he needed
something to get his life started. Stuart took a sip from
the glass at the foot of the couch and listened to a
young, wigless Elton John telling him that it was
"lonely out in space".

No lonelier than anywhere else, he thought. Yes, he
needed something, but he didn't know what it was.

He heard the doorbell and watched the colour drain
from his mother's face as she stammered, "Oh, I
wonder who that could be."

Stuart wondered if it was going to be an
intervention. He knew his aunts had been calling, knew
his mother had seen them on Sunday, coming back
red-eyed and tired and saying cattily that she'd like to
light a few candles, so he'd best not sigh so much, or
the place might go up in flames.

He heard a familiar voice, very unfamiliar to this
apartment. It seemed what his mother thought he
needed was Graham. He must *really* be in bad shape.

"Hello, Mother."

"Graham. Nice to see you."

"Likewise, Mother."

Graham had always called Glyniss "Mother". She was sure he did it to irritate her, to embarrass her in front of the world. Happy children didn't call their mothers Mother. It was Mom or Mammy or Mum. Mother was reserved for distant, imperious women, those who ordered, not reared. No one wanted to be called Mother. Mother was a big "Fuck You". Stuart always called her Ma.

They stood another moment in the door, Glyniss unconsciously blocking entry with an arm on the doorframe. She took a breath as if to speak but released it in a sigh.

"May I come in?" Graham asked so politely that Stuart flinched.

"Oh, yes… What a question! You can always come in. It's your home too," his mother replied, jumping out of the way and looking at the floor as she said it.

Excruciating, thought Stuart. But Graham said nothing and walked passed her into the living room, taking a seat across from Stuart.

"I hear your life's in the toilet, Stu."

"Now, I never said that, Graham," Glyniss said primly. "We just, that is Aunt Agathe and I just, well, Auntie Helen too, well, I just said I was worried to see Stuart so unhappy."

"I'm here to talk to you about getting yourself together a little here, bud," Graham said, seemingly ignoring his mother's stammering, but softening his approach just a little. He did like his older brother, even though he had a world of reasons not too.

"Well, I guess you are Mr. Fixit, aren't you," replied
Stuart. He regretted it instantly.

Graham was a carpenter. "Handyman" Glyniss
called him. He hadn't gone to school for it, just had the
natural ability and lucked into working with a good
craftsman. He'd done very well for himself, but it
wasn't the expected career path for a Lewis man. He
had eschewed bland offices and button-down shirts
and delusions of greater things to come, instead
spending his time making beautiful things with his
strong, hardened hands, things that left Stuart feeling
fey and inadequate. Cheap shots were his only counter.

Graham just smiled. "Well, your tongue ain't
busted," he said, falling into the stereotype, feeling no
shame. He would do it to drive his mother crazy. He
did it because he didn't care what they thought of him.
His had been a childhood more endured than
embraced. He'd had to get through it, and working
with his hands was how he'd done it, hiding away in
the shed in the back garden, until Glyniss had sold the
house. It was the reason he hadn't run away at sixteen
or ended up in jail or wrapped himself around a tree
seeping oil and blood on its roots. His work had saved
his life, and he was good at it and proud of it and
didn't need anybody to tell him he should be.

Glyniss responded to the exchange with a smile so
tight, it threatened to crack her face. "Oh, you boys.
Well I think I might just head out for a while and let
you two talk," she said through the grin. It was a little
grotesque, but Stuart had to give her credit for trying.

Once she had left, the brothers looked at each other
across what felt like miles before Graham shook his

head, repeating, "Oh, you boys," and started to laugh. Stuart joined in, and in a minute, they were roaring. A laugh full of wheezing and hooting and tears rolling down their cheeks. It was one of two ways of cutting the stress in the Lewis house, howls of rage or laughter.

"I can't believe you're here. They must be on suicide watch or something," Stuart said finally.

"Yeah, kind of. I can't believe *you're* here. God, what are you doing?"

"She threw me out."

"I heard. What'd you do?"

What had he done? No one had asked him that yet. Elizabeth and his mom had both taken the stance that the action was Emily's, so the blame was Emily's. Stuart quite liked that stance and had no intention of probing into what possible sins he might have committed to bring about his lover's change of heart.

"I didn't know where else to go."

"Elizabeth's? Agathe's? Hell, I would have thought you'd call me and Jane first."

"Yeah, but…"

"But?

"She doesn't, you know, expect anything from me." He realized it as he said it. There was no time to pretty it up.

"The hell she doesn't."

"She lets me be."

"She lets you be, all right. Be sad and pathetic and drunk. That's the way she likes us best. Listen, Stu, I'm sure you're upset about Emily, but this isn't doing you any good."

"You're not being fair. You'd damn Mom for

nothing. I don't have the same problems with her that you do. It's not my fault that she worries about me. She's supporting me."

"Oh, for Christ's sake, Stuart, supporting you? In lethargy and self-pity and drinking in the morning. Doesn't that strike you as a little bit familiar?"

"It was the easiest place to catch my breath."

"And are you catching it?"

"I'm…surviving."

Graham stood up from his seat, almost propelled from it. He wasn't a big talker and didn't have much patience for the gentle excuses his brother and mother made for themselves.

"Oh, come off it. Surviving? You're subsisting at best. You're not pulling yourself together here. You're just killing time."

That was how Graham worked. He never took offence at a comment about himself or his trade. A flip remark about his wife would get your nose bloodied, but aside from that, he didn't care what you said about him. He preferred you think him stupid. It only served to make you feel more like an asshole when he'd let loose a string of words so eloquent and insightful you were shamed to have to speak next. Graham was fucking brilliant.

Stuart watched, awed, as his brother paced the living room and continued to strip him of all excuses and feelings of entitlement.

"Do you think your life's over, Stuart? It's not. It's not on hold either. It's not waiting for you to come around here. It's happening as we speak."

"I just don't know what I'm supposed to be doing

now. You know? I thought I was supposed to be marrying Em, living downtown, working on websites and making my art. If that's not it, I've got to take the time now to figure out what it is I'm supposed to do. We don't all know at seventeen, Graham. We're not all like you."

Graham sighed and sat back down, rubbing his hand down his face as he did so and looking like the older brother he'd always had to be.

"Yeah, well, you're a little older than seventeen now, aren't you, buddy? So maybe it's not about what you're supposed to do any more, it's what you are going to do. At some point you're going to have to make a choice or give up entirely. Nothing will be perfect, but I guarantee you anything would be a step up from this. Dude, you are a thirty-three-year-old living at your mother's."

"Lots of people my age still live with their mothers. It's a new trend. I read about it in the paper."

"Yeah, well, maybe their mothers are fine, but we are talking about *our* mother. You don't even see what's happening here, do you? Have you looked at yourself lately? Have you seen what you're wearing?" Graham said, pointing at the pajamas and robe Stuart was wearing. "She got those for you, didn't she?"

"Yeah, so?"

"Doesn't your ensemble look a little familiar to you?"

Stuart, who hadn't been giving much thought to his appearance, ran his eyes down his own body; tan pajamas with the navy stripe, matching top and bottom. On his feet, leatherette slippers crossed at the front. The kind worn by old Italian men. And, oh shit… The kind worn by his father. She'd dressed him up like his father, who'd left the family for a newer, younger model in the mid-eighties. The one nobody really spoke to, or about, since his mother had sent the divorce papers to wherever it was he'd gone to.

"Holy shit."

"Yeah, man, it's creepy. And with that great unwashed thing you've got going on, it's even creepier. Just tuck that 26er in the crook of your elbow, and it's Sunday at the Lewis's, 75-84."

Stuart looked at himself one more time, than looked up at his brother, and in that instant, Stuart remembered how to make a decision.

"Dude, I've got to find my own apartment."

*　　*　　*

Kate enjoyed unemployment immensely. She loved waking up early, knowing that she didn't have to. She drank in the long rays of her daylight hours, not the least bit afraid that she wouldn't be able to fill them. There's always something to do—clean a closet, take a walk, spot paint the chips on the baseboards. By the time she got up, bathed and dressed, it would be nearly time to make breakfast. And by the time she'd cooked and eaten and read the papers and had her coffee, it was usually very nearly time to start thinking about lunch.

Whenever Kate had been without work, she could not imagine how she even managed to function when she was working. It takes time to treat yourself humanely, and when you are working, you never seem to have any. When you work, instead of bathing, you hose yourself

off. You forgo cooking in favour of shovelling spoonfuls
of canned vegetables into your mouth. Your clothes are
housed on the floor, where you can grab the least
rumpled thing off the pile and wear it out in public. Kate
could admit it. She knew she had sniffed at the armpits of
her sweaters, she knew she had spritzed perfume on the
crotch of her jeans to get away with wearing them
another day. She had lived like an animal, sniffing and
pawing at her things. It was uncivilized.

But in the end, it was necessary. Kate knew she had
to go ask for a job to do, then do it. She'd never really
thought too much about what she wanted to do. What
she wanted to do was not work. Who in their right
mind would want anything else? But she did like her
apartment, and now that she was going to have to pay
the rent all on her own again, she would have to find
herself some type of employment.

It was only because Scott had left her two month's
rent in lieu of notice that she'd been able to have any
time off at all. Everyone was scandalized that she had
taken it. She supposed she should be too. After all, he
hadn't wanted to go, it had been her idea. But when
he'd offered her this rental reprieve in that Christian
martyr-y turn-the-other-cheek manner of his, she
couldn't help but think she deserved it, just for having
to listen to him.

But it was November now, and with the holidays
coming, she really did need a job. Actually, what she
really thought she needed was a new boyfriend. The
holidays are a hell of a time to be alone. But without a
job, it was nearly impossible to get yourself a
boyfriend.

You could find men, no problem, she'd discovered, thanks to the wondrous invention of the Internet. She'd tried in the last few weeks to get back on that horse, creating profiles for herself on various dating sites, the ones she'd always pitied her single friends for using. She'd used a nice photo with a nice shot of her breasts and had received a fair number of "winks"—requests to email. But once she'd agreed to contact them, things always headed quickly downhill. The Instant Messaging window generally read something like this:

Hi I'm Accomplished Stockbroker (Fun-Loving Surf Bum, Big hearted father of two etc. etc.)

Hi I'm Kate

You look nice in your photo Kate

Thanks, so do you

So, What do you do all day Kate?

-- ---- ----- ----- Nothing.

This was where the conversation could vary. Some wrote "Oh", some said "No, seriously, where do you work". Others didn't respond at all.

The same would happen when she and her sister or Megan would head out for a drink in the evening. Eyes would meet, drinks would be offered, and things would hum along right up until Kate mentioned she was unemployed. Then, almost without fail, her suitor would turn about three inches to Kate's right, somehow forget she was still there and introduce himself to her friends.

It was an unfortunate side effect of female liberation, Kate thought, that a man could now judge an unemployed woman as harshly as she judged unemployed men.

There was no getting around it. To have a boyfriend, Kate needed to find a job. Although common thought would lead you to think differently, Kate didn't expect it would be that hard. Kate had never had trouble finding a new job. What she lacked in work ethic and experience, she made up for in connections.

Her father had been a CPA for years, a good one. He had in the past always managed to put a good word in the right ear to get Kate an interview. Once she was in the door, she could handle things. She was friendly, she was confident and pretty, but not in an impending harassment suit kind of way. Kate looked capable.

Now that she had split with Scott, however, and been fired from another job, she found her dad unwilling to sully his name any more by associating it with hers.

"I'm worried about you, cookie, but I just can't help you here. There's no one left to call."

Kate told him that it was okay; she didn't think she was cut out for finance anyway. She wanted something new.

Not too new, however. As much as she saw this as an opportunity to reinvent herself, she wasn't about to end up serving coffee to the people she used to work with or anything. How mortifying.

So when Megan had offered to put Kate's name forward to become the next administrative assistant to one Jennifer Davies, of the family law firm Davies and Associates, Kate had accepted. Megan had been working there a few years and was considered a star player. Her word was enough to secure Kate an interview, even with her somewhat sketchy employment history and lack of law experience.

She was torn about the opportunity. While happy to have landed an interview so easily, and in a posh office right downtown near all the good shopping, she worried about the consequences of not doing well. She knew Megan was worried too. She knew, because Megan had told her so.

"I want to help you here, Katie, and I think you'd be really good at dealing with Jennifer. But I have to tell you this, with a lot of love, okay? If you get this job and fuck it up, it's going to look really bad on me. And if you make me look bad at work, I will find a way to kill you and make it look like a very embarrassing accident."

Kate knew it was unwise to take a job under these conditions. Friends and work are a worse mix even than work and sex. She knew if she screwed up, she'd lose a lot more than just her paycheque, but she kind of hoped that the fear of messing up might be what she needed to stick to it, to come in every day and try. If she even got the job in the first place.

She was determined to do her best. She had managed to peel herself out of bed at the ungodly hour of six thirty to wash, shave and beautify herself, leaving ample time to reconsider the outfit she'd picked for the occasion. Grey pencil skirt, white button-down shirt, black v-neck sweater. She hated blazers. She thought they made her look like a twelve-year-old girl and a linebacker at the same time. When her friends were being honest with her, they agreed.

It was good. She finished with textured black tights and very pointy, very high heels, which she'd learned to walk in, even though they killed her feet, because the woman on *What Not to Wear* told her to.

After she'd dressed, stepping carefully, so carefully into her tights, she scraped her blonde hair back into a low ponytail and took stock. How did she look?

Professional, she decided. Crisp. She looked like a grown-up, which never ceased to thrill her, as she spent most of her time feeling like a camp counsellor. She didn't wear make-up, since she didn't want to chance a bad result. She topped the whole thing off with a slim black purse and the trench coat she'd picked up from an outlet across the border in the summer. She walked out of the apartment feeling like she'd just finished the most successful game of dress-up ever.

Kate got to the firm early enough to have a coffee in the shop in the lobby, collect her thoughts and pee three times. She always had to pee, but even more when she was nervous. She was not the kind of girl you wanted to go to the movies with.

By the time she had announced herself at the front desk, she felt like she'd emptied her bladder of drinks she hadn't even had yet, and yet the urge was still there. She'd never felt so unsure about an interview before. She guessed it was because she had never really cared before if she got the job.

At eight thirty precisely, she was brought into a long, narrow conference room and left to sit alone with her thoughts until shortly before nine; just enough time for her to become nearly beside herself with panic. She could hear her heart hammering in her ears, her breath coming out in short bursts. She knew her cheeks and ears were burning. It was ridiculous, but when the door actually opened, she thought she might faint.

A tall, sharp-featured brunette popped her head in the door. "You're Katherine Mackenzie?"

Kate nodded.

"A friend of Megan Fields?"

Another nod.

"Have you ever been in conflict with the law, Katherine?"

A shake of the head.

"Okay. Well, I need someone who can type and take minutes and handle my phone calls and not bug the hell out of me while they do it. And I need someone who'll do it for $35,000. Are you that person, Katherine?"

Nod.

"Good then, there's some papers to fill out at the front desk, and you can start on Monday. I loathe interviewing people." And with that, she walked out of the room. Returning almost immediately, the brunette asked, "You *are* capable of talking, aren't you, Katherine?"

"Uh-huh."

"We're good then. See you Monday."

The door closed behind her, and Kate was left to stare around the office, trying to determine what had just happened. Megan found her there shortly after, still seated, still clutching the copy of the résumé she'd brought.

"So you got it!"

"I think so."

"Yeah, she just told me. Congratulations!"

"Thanks. Can I ask you something stupid?"

"History has proven that indeed you can."

"Hah. It's just. That woman. That was her, right? That's my boss?"

"Yeah, that's Jennifer."

"Just checking." Then Kate took a breath, grabbed her coat, walked with Megan to the front desk and signed on to work for a woman who scared the shit out of her.

December

Stuart had been given fair warning that tackling the holidays alone was going to be a nightmare.

The holidays are awful without someone to love, they said. He tended to counter that the holidays were awful anyway, since even when he and Emily had been together, he had been the underemployed wunderkind who had never truly explored his potential...just ask his third grade art teacher. But they smiled knowingly, telling him that it could, and would get, worse.

Who were *they?* Well, his mother to start. A woman somewhat defeated by life who knew firsthand the misery a solitary Christmas brought. A woman who was half sorry her son would go through it, and half glad that he was finally going to understand what she had endured the last twenty years without slitting her wrists. Maybe Stuart would be a little more understanding about why she'd never baked perfect Christmas cookies or stood in line at the mall for forty hours to let a wino in a red suit fondle her children while promising them the moon.

They also included his Aunt Helen, who was never shy to explain to her nephew that "The perfect person is not an angel down from heaven, son. It's the person you were meant to be with, not the person you wish you could be with." She knew this from hard experience, having found her soulmate in a man who could scream as loud, sulk as long and laugh as hard as she could.

Also represented on this list was his best friend Elizabeth and her shiny new husband. Liz said the only good reason she could think of for getting married was that people would stop referring to Michael as her "life partner". The two had fallen into a relationship by freak accident and decided they liked it there. "I can't believe that knocking up a woman I barely knew is the proudest accomplishment of my life, but I'm telling you, in my case it was the key to the Kingdom. Seriously guy, you should try it."

Then of course, there was Emily, who had not returned one of his calls in the first three months of their break-up, reducing him to a serial hang-up artist after leaving his fiftieth pleading message. She who had not made one attempt at contacting him, until one bright December afternoon, a greeting card with "My Christmas Includes Kwanzaa" embossed on the front slipped through the mail slot of his new apartment. It informed him that she was in a new relationship and that she hoped he could find it within himself to get over her and on with his own life, since "It's a big world out there to navigate alone, Stu." Oh, and she also wished him all the best in the New Year. He still thought she was a bit of a cunt.

But even with all of these naysayers, Stuart was feeling okay. Good even, better than he had been. There is some comfort in the certainty that you are about to endure a truly shit time. To know that nothing you can do or say can improve your chance at happiness and that the stars are aligned against you makes hoping for more impossible. That soothed him. Reality won't break your heart. Reality you can medicate for; it's hope that will break your heart.

Armed with this knowledge and a ridiculously large bottle of very poor quality vodka, Stuart leapt into the holiday fracas. First stop, Elizabeth's office Christmas party.

Stuart had been attending Liz's office party for years as her quasi-date and felt that this year should be no different, recent acquisition of a baby-daddy be damned. (The only other good reason Elizabeth had for getting married was to stop people from calling Michael her "baby-daddy".)

"Why do you want to go to this thing? *I* don't even want to go to this thing," she said when he had asked her the date of the party so he could keep his calendar clear.

"You're only saying that because you're pregnant. I'm not the one who gave up my free drink tickets for the thrill of procreation. That was your choice. Why should I be punished?"

"If it's free drinks you're after, why don't you just come by the house some night?"

"Because, Liz, it's not just the drinks, it's…the whole thing."

Stuart loved Liz's office. The organized drudgery seemed exotic to him. People went there every day, for years. They spent this unfathomably large part of their lives in a place with grey carpets, grey walls and the occasional plastic plant tucked in a corner, and they had all acclimatized to it. They just accepted the banality. Except at Christmas, when the place let loose in a frenzy of well-mandated chaos that made Stuart want to wet himself laughing.

Liz's boss was old-school in her celebrations. No parties at a lakefront hotel and group donations to African charities for Davies and Associates. It was strictly cheese platters and baked goods brought in by staff, tinsel and wine by the box and ten-dollar-limit gift swap gags. There was something so refreshingly middle-America about it. You wouldn't be surprised to see a gelatin mold wobbling to the beat of the Boney M tune pounding from the portable CD player.

But Jennifer Davies was also a lawyer, and this was the bit that made the party a highlight of Stuart's year. He couldn't get enough of the plastic mistletoe and the accompanying posted letter about harassment. The desks were piled high with trees and Santas and menorahs and nativity scenes all vying for holiday supremacy. Jennifer even played the "fireplace DVD", a two-hour movie featuring a Yule log burning, and burning, and burning on the boardroom's monitors to keep any undisclosed pagans happy.

The energy that pumped through this little office rested on the knife's edge of celebration or subpoena. It was palpable, and the more drinks consumed, the looser tongues got, and the atmosphere became downright electric. This was a night that a conversation about recent senate changes could end with a drink in the face or a tumble in the backseat of someone's expensive, though fuel-efficient, hybrid SUV.

"Come on, Lizzie, it's better than HBO."

"It's great to hear how my life provides you with

such amusement. Ass. Anyway, maybe Michael wants to come with me."

"You're going to take Mike to the party?"

"Well, he is the father of my fetus, Stu. It'd be a bit weird to take another date to my work party, you know?"

"Did I hear my name?" Michael said, walking into the room.

"Your life partner here; yeah that's right, I said it, your LIFE PARTNER is trying to ditch me and take you to her office party," Stuart responded a little more sulkily than he had intended.

He desperately wanted to go to this thing. He was thirty-three years old, alone, and desperate to go to his newly married best friend's office party.

"Oh, come on, Ellie," said Michael. He called her Ellie, even though it wasn't a short form for Elizabeth, and there were like thousands to choose from, Liz, Liza, Betty, Lilibet, etc. Stuart had grown to like him in spite of this, though truthfully it had taken a while. "Let him go with you. If I can't make a sacrifice for a guy alone for the holidays, what kind of dick am I? And by sacrifice, I mean no sacrifice at all, because Christmas parties are lame."

Since there was a large part of Stuart which wanted very much to tell Mike that he was probably the kind of dick who is always flaccid and bent to the left, he was mildly surprised to hear himself say, "See, he doesn't want to go, Ellie. Come on!"

Oh god, he was begging. Was that the only way he could talk to women these days? He saw her face soften and knew she pitied him a bit. But that was fine, if pity was what was going to change her mind.

"Okay, yes, we'll go, Stu. It'll be fun."

"And by fun, she means a gigantic pain in her ass," added Michael jovially.

"Did you just say I have a huge ass?" snapped Elizabeth, turning towards him.

Before he could answer, Stuart said a quick goodbye and headed for the door, thanking whichever god it was that had invented karmic revenge.

* * *

"It's not too slutty. It's just slutty enough," Megan had decided.

"I'd kind of prefer not to look slutty at all, Meg," Kate said, spinning in front of the mirror so as to detect any wayward flashes of bra peeping out from the dress's wide neckline.

"I'd kind of like it if you stopped referring to all of the clothes in my wardrobe as 'slutty,'" Tracy piped in, holding the last discarded halter top to her chest like a baby.

"Sorry, I mean I'd like to look office-appropriate," said Kate, bending forward to see what might fall out if she leaned in for a drink or something off the food table. "Don't you think it's still too much?"

"Well, why don't you just throw on a turtleneck and tweed skirt and be done with it," snapped Tracy, tired of watching her sister strut around the bedroom in various garments. "You came over here because you wanted party clothes, and I hate to tell you, but this is what party clothes look like."

"I know, I know, but it's just I'm new there, you know. I don't want to look stupid. Meg, what do you think? You're the one that got me the job. Will I shame you if I go looking like this?"

"Not at all. You will, however, shame me, and yourself, if you get piss-drunk and make a run at one of the techies."

Biting her tongue again (it was a wonder she had any of it left), Kate managed to say nothing and look sheepish, as was expected. Having spent the last two months on a hysterical manhunt so that she would have a boyfriend to take to her parents' for the holidays, Kate had ended up with nothing but an extra ten pounds of liquor weight and irritated friends. She was in no position to demand that she be treated any better.

"Sorry, sorry, I'm not your mother," said Megan. She was one of the few people Kate knew that could recognize when she had actually caused offence and was willing to apologize for it. It was a true gift.

"She does a pretty good imitation though, eh, Katie?" Tracy said to lighten the mood. Tracy was never one for contemplative silences, or silence of any kind.

"So I've got a dress, some shoes and your orders to behave like a lady. Now what the hell am I going to do with my hair?"

"Pony tail, smooth one," said Megan with authority. "Fancy dress, simple hair. It's trying too hard that makes you look slutty, ladies."

*　　*　　*

Stuart woke up with a dry mouth and a pounding head

but in his own bed. Making it home, a good sign. He sat up to find that he was sitting in his clothes, and that his pillowcase was covered in vomit. Puking in your sleep, a bad sign.

Three p.m. He had an hour to decide to live, shower and get to his great aunt's for his family Christmas party. Knowing that Agathe's particular brand of ice-cold hostility was worse than the fear of vomiting on the subway, he rolled out of bed and into the shower. Wrapping a towel around himself as he finished, he grabbed the Febreeze, doused his encrusted pillow and sheets and headed towards the closet, thinking about the night before and trying to decide if he'd had a good time.

It was hard to say for sure. The evening had taken on an unreal quality quite early. He'd spent the first hour of the party listening to Elizabeth's colleagues tell him that they had known that she and Stuart would wind up together one day. Soulmates and all that. Then he watched their expressions change as a red-faced Elizabeth explained that he was not, in fact, the husband she had recently acquired, and that that man couldn't be there tonight because of total disinterest, er, important business.

As word spread that the pregnant Elizabeth had brought an old boyfriend to the party, it was as though she and Stuart were emitting some sort of force field that people would butt up against but could not penetrate. It shifted as they walked the room, to the bar, the buffet or the bathroom. They could have swung a metre stick in any direction and not hit anything.

"I knew this was going to be a bad idea," she whispered at him through her teeth.

"Better stop that, it looks like you're blowing sweet nothings at me."

"Fuck off."

"No, you fuck off."

It was strange and uncomfortable, but honestly more for Elizabeth. Stuart kind of liked it. He was one half of a couple again, even if it was an odd couple. People were seeing him as part of a set. And he had always loved Elizabeth in his way. Sad and misinterpreted as it was, it was a connection at least.

He rooted around the back of the closet, looking for one of the button-down shirts his mother gave him whenever a gift-giving opportunity provided her the chance. He never wore them, but today he thought he'd give her a thrill. He wanted a "do the right thing" moment to balance out the fact that last night he'd revelled in his friend's discomfort and slept in his own filth.

He wasn't even sure why he had gotten so drunk. Well, yes, he was. He did it because he could. Because drinking was an activity, so if he was drinking, he was doing something. It was what he did instead of talking to the people at the party or dancing with Elizabeth or crying when U2's "Baby Please Come Home" came on…

Or "Blue Christmas"…

Or "I'll Be Home for Christmas".

That one had almost ruined him. But then it always had. Even when he'd been with Emily. Even when he'd been happy.

What was it about Christmas songs that just gutted you? All happiness and good tidings carried through your ear canal on melodies that just split you right open. And heaven help you if you happened to be looking at a string of lights or a baby or your lover when you heard it. The human heart wasn't meant to think too much on the wonders of this world, because the human mind can only think of what it would be like to lose them. Better to crawl around in your life's despair than to call the gods' attentions to your joys, to show the world your soft underbelly.

So he drank his face off and watched the parade. The men back-slapping and glad-handing, the women dancing to eighties music and laughing softly at themselves and at each other. Wanting to be looked at, but not sure by whom. They looked good, some of them. They had tried. Made an effort. Stuart liked that about them. Made him feel special, though Lord knows they hadn't done it for him. Not intentionally. He looked among them, trying to decide which of the young ones he'd talk to, if he was going to talk to any of them; which he wasn't. Maybe the one in the shiny jeans? She looked like fun. Perhaps the one with the backless dress? She looked easy. But also fierce. No, he couldn't talk to a girl like that. All that skin exposed, all that confidence. If she looked right at him, his brain might melt. Maybe the one in the sparkly black dress in the corner, her hair tied back with a red ribbon. She seemed like the kind of girl you could talk to. If you were the kind of guy who could talk to girls.

"Who is that?" he said to Elizabeth, jerking his head to the corner.

"Who? Oh, her. I don't know her name, she's new. Jenn's assistant or something," Elizabeth replied tiredly. She'd been bored since she got there; sober, hormonal, embarrassed, bloated and bored. Then she sat up with a glint in her eye. "Why, do you want to talk to her?"

"No, Yente, I don't want to talk to her. I was just, she just, she looks…nice."

"Well, if you are not going to talk to anybody, and we are just going to sit here getting stared at for the rest of the night, I declare you victorious in your battle with Ernest and Julio, and I say we go home."

Which they did, he now remembered. He'd rolled in at a ridiculously early hour. Eleven-ish, and he'd been fine. Drunk but fine. It was the next three hours spent drinking vodka out of a coffee mug that had gotten him in trouble. He was going to have to start watching that.

Dressed, he walked into the living room to pick up the gifts he'd bought for the family, spying in the corner the DVD player he'd bought himself. He picked it up too and added it to the pile. His brother didn't have one. Come to think of it, Stuart wasn't even sure if Graham had a TV. But he was getting it all the same, for all he'd done helping Stuart out from under his mother and getting his place in order. Stuart counted it as another check in his good person column.

*   *   *

"How was the party, Katie?" said Tracy in lieu of a greeting.

Kate hopped in the car and took a few minutes to arrange her coat and bag and thoughts before responding. "It was okay. It was fine. I survived it."

"Yeah, that sounds amazing."

"No, it was good. It was, well it was what it always is. What I should have expected. I don't know why I thought it'd be…"

"Magic?"

"Yeah, magic."

"Well, Kate, that's because you had the misfortune of being born a girl. You got all dressed up for the ball and ended up at the office," Tracy said, pulling away from the curb and heading towards a Mackenzie family Christmas.

"Pretty much. It was stupid."

"Well, don't blame yourself," Tracy reassured her. "Blame Walt effin' Disney."

"Effin'? Seriously?"

"I'm practicing so I'll win the best daughter award at the end of this. Now that Scott's gone, the field is really wide open."

"Hah."

"So aside from the inevitable let down, anything good happen?"

"Not really."

"C'mon Katie, we've got a three-hour drive ahead of us. Better dig up something light to talk about, or else we'll have to start discussing our 'feelings', and frankly I like to save the airing of the grievances for when we are all together."

"Good point. Ummm, well it was kind of tacky, actually. They served stuff like cubed cheddar and wheat crackers. Oh, and you'll love this, the wine was straight out of the box."

"You're not serious."

"Yeah. But at least you could serve yourself. Meg and I got 'white wine wasted.'" This was a Mackenzie family term describing the head-achy, mildly nauseous dry-mouthed effect of one too many glasses of

Chardonnay. "I slept till noon today and had to drink, like, six gallons of water. So be prepared to stop, a lot, on the way."

"Oh, Christ, what's new? Speaking of new, anybody interesting at the party?"

"Well, I talked to a few people in the office but mostly kept my mouth shut and hung with Meg. People are big time gossipy at Davies and Associates. Lawyer-client privilege, my ass. Heard some case talk and met Jennifer's husband. He's ridiculously rich, they say."

"Ummm, by anybody I meant men, and by your response, I'm guessing no."

"No. Not really. Everyone in my office is old. Well, the men, anyway. There was one younger guy there that was kind of cute. But he came with one of the lawyers. One who's married and pregnant, but he's not her husband, apparently."

"Really? Weird."

"Yeah. Rumour is she was single forever, then, like a few weeks ago, she showed up at the office telling everyone she'd married some guy and was pregnant. No one even knew she was seeing anyone. They thought they'd meet him at the party."

"And she showed up with another guy?"

"Yeah. Apparently he comes with her every year. An old boyfriend or something? Everyone started congratulating him on upcoming fatherhood and stuff. It was pretty funny."

"And he was the most eligible guy at the party?"

"Yeah."

"The guy who takes his married, pregnant ex-girlfriend out on dates."

"Yeah."

"God help us all. Hey, have you still got Scottie's number? Since you're done with him, maybe I'll call and wish him a Happy New Year. At least he's got a house."

"Fuck off, Tracy."

"And so it begins," Tracy said, satisfied, and turned up the radio.

✳   ✳   ✳

The house was full of the smell of pine. It didn't come from the majestic tree standing in the corner, lights all a-twinkle. That tree was plastic. It came instead straight from the nozzle of Christmas in a Can, an air "enhancer" Aunt Agathe had assaulted every room in the house with.

When Stuart asked her why she hadn't just ordered a real tree, she'd sniffed, "The great outdoors is best left there." Then she'd told him not to be bold, slapped his cheek lightly and told him she could still smell the liquor on him, but chuckled as he'd handed her the requisite bouquet of white roses.

"The Asians think white is a colour of mourning. Must make winter a pretty crap time for them, hey?" Uncle Henry's voice came booming across the foyer with a comment as sure to come as the sunrise. Stuart shuddered internally every time he heard it, but needed it now to convince himself this was home.

"Never thought of that before, Uncle Henry," said Stuart, slipping off his coat and handing it to the young housekeeper employed by his aunt. "Sorry," he said to her as she took it from him. He always said that, and he couldn't quite look her in the eye.

"What are you sorry for?" snapped Agathe. "That's what I pay you for, isn't it, Margaret?"

"Yes, Mrs. Davidson," Margaret replied. Not unpleasantly. She didn't think that her job was shameful or unfair. Only Stuart thought that, and they both knew it. Finding he couldn't crawl out of his skin, Stuart made instead for the living room, dodging children hopped up on sugar and fantasies, and scanned the room for his mother.

He saw her sitting on the sofa, an uncomfortable smile on her face. Glyniss didn't like family gatherings. She didn't like to be the divorcée, the mother of two non-professional sons, the grandmother of nobody, the secretary, the high school graduate, herself.

"Happy Holidays, Ma," said Stuart, bending over to kiss her cheek, then remembering his aunt's admonishment, pulling back at the last second to kiss the top of her head instead. He could taste the spray she used to keep her curls in place, the perfume she used to skip a wash and save her from having to roll her hair each night.

"You're late, Stuart. And you look awful. Are you unwell?"

"Just tired, that's all. Out a bit late last night."

"With a young lady?" she asked, ever hopeful.

"Sort of," he smiled. "Does a pregnant married lady count?"

"Oh. Elizabeth. No."

Stuart dropped on the couch beside her and kissed her on the cheek anyway. He knew he had her. He could feel her relax a bit into the chair.

"I have your presents. Want them now, or want to wait until morning?"

His mother could never wait for anything. "Opening one wouldn't hurt, I guess," she said, bolstered and now the proud mother of a son thoughtful enough to buy her presents. She loved presents. They were attention in a box, and she could never get enough. "Oh," she said, a bit deflated. "I suppose we should wait for Graham?"

It was a question, not a statement; the duty line required in the good mother handbook. He knew what he was supposed to say.

"I don't think he'd mind, Ma."

It was all she needed. "Well, okay then, just the one."

They started with the small ones, lavender hand cream from the fancy French bath store, a gift certificate from her favourite women's clothing shop, slippers. Until all that was left was the DVD player in the corner. Still no Graham.

"Is that for your brother?"

"Yes."

"What is it?"

"A DVD player."

"My. I bet that was quite expensive."

"Well, not too much."

"Still. You don't think…"

"Think what, Ma?"

"You don't think he'd, you know, sell it…for drugs?"

Ridiculous as it was, the question didn't surprise Stuart. It did make him sad.

"He's not a drug addict, Ma." He told her quietly.

"I know what I saw."

"What you saw? You mean that joint? In his school bag, like, fifteen years ago? I think that's probably just about out of his bloodstream by now," he said, trying to sound funny but feeling the edge in his voice.

"Don't make fun, Stuart. I worry because I care. I'm just glad I never had to worry about you."

Stuart had a wild moment where he thought he might mention that he'd have been a lot later if he'd pulled the vomit stained sheets off his bed before heading to the party instead of letting them crust into the mattress.

But he didn't. Of course he didn't. He had these moments sometimes. Favourite child's remorse, a strange guilt at having been anointed the better son through absolutely no merit of his own. They always passed.

"Well, anyway," his mother sniffed, "it was very good of you."

"Graham helped me find my place. Did a lot of repair work on it too."

"Of course he did, Stuart. That's what brothers do."

* * *

By the time they had rolled into the driveway of their parents' house, Kate and Tracy were hoarse from singing along to the oldies rock station they'd picked up when they'd finally made it outside of the city. After the initial hour of one-sided conversation, where Tracy tried to make Kate admit she was being a giant suck for not getting over her Scott comment, "which was an effin' joke, man", Kate had been forced to break her silence by the sheer joy she felt at being in a part of the province that could still appreciate the musical genius of the Northern Pikes.

No matter what differences in temperament and personality the two sisters had, they would be forever united by the sweet time warp of northern FM radio. AM radio back in the day.

By the time they had left Teenland, the two had silently agreed a truce had been reached and that it would be best maintained if they kept singing and stayed away from any conversation that didn't revolve around trying to remember who sang which parts in "Tears Are Not Enough".

Waiting for the garage door to open and let them in, Kate stared at the string of lights edging the front door and felt surprisingly cheerful. Her trips home usually began with a sense of failure, because no matter how hard she tried, she could not seem to stop the regression to her seventeen-year-old self every time she crossed the entranceway.

Her voice would take on a whine that made her cringe. She would roll her eyes and stretch out all vowels (Mooooom, Daaaaaad, coooome ooooooooon), and she would feel strange and awkward if she ran into old school acquaintances or teachers at the mall or the post office, still thinking it was inappropriate to be seeing them outside of the classroom setting.

Once she hit home, she could not stop herself from thinking how weird it was that friends who'd stayed behind were now married to people she'd never have dared/deigned to talk to ten years ago. She would go and visit her best friend from grade school, and while she was listening to all of the local happenings and cooing at the babies, Kate couldn't help thinking, *You seriously and on a regular basis look at Jody Donaldson's thing? And like, don't laugh?*

But this time, seeing the lights casting long, fuzzy shadows on the snow, she didn't mind feeling a bit like a kid. In a way, she *was* still a kid. Free and unencumbered, unsure of what to do next, she'd tossed off her first try at adulthood and hadn't found another style to fit, so home really was the place to be.

Plus, Kate really did love Christmas, all the sparkle and twinkle.

Tracy pulled the car into the garage, narrowly avoiding the pile of old bikes and ski equipment that lined the sides. She waited to hear the last few strains of "Rockin' Santa", or "Santa Loves to Rock", or "Rock With Me Santa"…one of those Christmas Carol monstrosities, then turned off the ignition. "Think we'll survive it?"

"Maybe just."

*   *   *

The liquor supply dwindled as the hours passed, but it was still much too early for anyone to get this upset. Unless that person was Henry. Dinner had not even been served yet, and Henry had gotten himself good and outraged. Even the thick blanket of aerosol pine smell could not smother it.

Something had his Irish up. Even from the other side of the party, Helen could see his index finger jabbing accusingly into Stuart's arm, rhythmically punctuating every point he was trying to make.

"How can anyone get themselves worked up like that? It's Christmas," Helen asked her daughter, gesturing toward the two of them and trying to determine if she liked her nephew enough to walk over and save him from the mono-digit assault.

"Stuart told him if they'd wanted three wise men for the party today, they could have recruited at the last Liberal convention, then they'd only have needed to look for another two and a half," said Lily, attempting to pry a Nanaimo bar out of her youngest child's tiny clutches.

"Oh well, the hell with him then," Helen said, dismissing the young man's pleading gazes. "He's brought this on himself."

"Except that if Dad keeps this up, he's going to have a heart attack, scarring your grandchildren for life," Lily said, grabbing the glass out of Helen's hand and pushing her gently towards the eye of the storm. "You can have this back when you've taken care of business."

Helen wanted to resist but couldn't help noticing the florid colouring of her husband's face, the mixture of too many vodka tonics and entirely too much investment in the defence of our nation's leaders.

"I'll have damn well earned it," she sighed, heading across the room.

"Watching you making this much of a public spectacle, I'd at least hope it would be in the defense of *my* honour," she said, stepping between the two men and quickly running a hand across Henry's forehead, wiping away the beads of sweat.

"Oh, these kids, Helen," Henry practically spat at her. "They think they know everything. They've never had to work for anything in their lives. Never had to fight for anything. Everything always just handed to them, then they bite the hands that feed them!"

She grabbed his hand just before he was about to land a jab.

"Don't even think about it. And quit yelling at me— I'm not one of the kids. Actually, quit yelling, full stop. This is Christmas, and you are supposed to be spending quality time with your family, so you had better just simmer down and enjoy it."

"I'm not yelling. I'm just trying to set this boy straight," Henry said, attempting to temper his anger.

"Honest to god, Henry…" she mumbled, then turned to Stuart, saying, "It's a miracle I haven't murdered this one yet."

But as the words left her lips, she took a look at her nephew and instantly regretted them. Seeing him standing there, lord of the manor, son of the adoring Glynnis, the cocky stance and indulgent smile, her irritation faded and turned into something else.

"You sure can get fired up about things there, Unc. Better watch your blood pressure. Ha! Ha!"

Ha Ha. So funny, this old uncle and crusty aunt; a regular comedy routine. So cute. Whatever affection this boy had for her Henry was laced with pity; pity for an old man with an old body and older notions. And pity for her. An old woman married to an old boor; one breast missing and a saggy ass to boot.

Helen realized if there was a man she'd gladly kill in this triangle, it wasn't Henry.

She proceeded to tell Stuart that, ensuring the point was hammered home with the tip of a well-manicured nail. "Well, aren't you clever? Isn't it delightful to be young and healthy and full of wisdom?"

"What?" said Stuart, surprised by her tone. "No. I was just…"

"Just what? Just thinking what a gas it is to mess with someone who is passionate about something? Passion. Must be quite exotic to you, huh? Mr. Apathy?" She was getting louder. She could hear herself getting louder than she meant to. She couldn't help it.

"No…I…Aunt Helen." Stuart knew he'd already lost this battle. Lost it before it started. Now he was just trying to find the most dignified way to go running from a fight with an old lady.

"What, nothing more to say? All tapped out on smartass?"

"I don't need anyone to defend me, Helen. I'm quite capable of…"

"Oh, shut it, Henry," she snapped. She was on fire here, and there was nothing to douse it. Best just stand back and let it burn out.

Everyone was actively looking at other things, and Stuart knew this was his time to get away. Before she locked his eyes again. But he was too late. She was staring at him again. Blazing. That's when he felt it coming. He knew it was wrong. He tried to smother it. He smirked. And Helen combusted.

"Oh, it's funny, is it? A cranky old lady defending a cranky old man? Well, I happen to love this man. Who is here to defend *you*, Stuart? Your mother? Who loves *you*?" With that, she was done. And so was he.

Stuart fell. Just like a house of cards, he toppled against the cool marble of the fireplace. He was leaning at first, just for a minute. Just to catch his breath. But he started to slide, and he kept going until he was sitting on the oak floor, sitting eye to saucer-eye with his three-year-old cousin Maxwell.

"Down, Stu?"

"Yeah, Max, I'm down."

Max looked at him, then around the room at all the grownups, and he sensed the fear. That something bad was about to happen.

"Grandma gonna spank you, Stu?" the little boy whispered, full of concern. He knew the injustice of being punished at Christmas.

"She already has," Stuart said, patting Max's head and attempting to maintain even the smallest shred of dignity in front of the people who loved him. Did they love him? His aunt sure as hell didn't. Not at that moment. Who *did* love him? He shouldn't have asked himself, because shortly after the question ran through his mind, and very much against his will, Stuart started to cry. Glynnis ran to him and put her arms around him, careful not to get caught in the crossfire of her sister's nuclear gaze.

The room was quiet, but not deathly so. This was awkward. It was uncomfortable, but it had happened before. This was what family did—Stuart's family, anyway. Vicious and upsetting as these set-tos could be, one had never finished them off yet. Battered and bruised, but never broken; it should have been on their family crest.

As everyone waited for the inevitable next move, they heard footsteps, then a voice.

"Crying brother, check. Crying mother, check. Distraught children, check. Merry Fucking Christmas. Glad I'm late."

"Actually, Graham," said Agathe, walking across the room and patting Jane's arm in greeting, "you are just in time. Helen will apologize to your brother, Stuart will apologize to your uncle, and you'll apologize to the room for such vulgar language. Then the turkey will be served. And Graham, where are my roses?"

*   *   *

"To be forced to get up early on a holiday morning is an assault on the human spirit."

This was the truth Kate woke up to early Christmas morning, delivered in the loud, agitated voice of her sister, who had walked into her room and crawled into bed with her, not even bothering to take off her boots, still dripping wet from an overnight downpour of snow.

"Well then," she mumbled, rolling away from the cold circling Tracy like an aura, "Stop assaulting me."

"Ha ha. You're the funny one. Get your ass up. I have already been up helping clean out the driveway so we can get the car out. And remember, it was your effin', no, screw it, fucking, it was your fucking idea to have us all get up for Christmas mass 'like a family'. I'm out there freezing my ass off, and you didn't even get up to put the fuckin' coffee on?

Kate sighed heavily before rolling over, saying, "Mmmm, coffee. Would you mind getting that on the go while I get ready?" She half-expected to be smothered to death by a pillow at that point and was thinking it wouldn't be such a terrible place to spend all eternity, her bed being one of her favourite places.

Surprisingly, Tracy hopped up and said "Okay,"

heading towards the door. Kate was almost back asleep when Tracy turned, and in two steps made it back to the bed, where she grabbed two fistfuls of blanket and yanked them clear off the bed, leaving Kate exposed to the effects of her father's frugality when it came to heating the house. She would have preferred the smothering.

"Do I look like a fucking housekeeper?" Tracy stalked out of the room, taking the blankets with her, calling back, "Get your ass up. Dad wants us out of here in, like, ten minutes. Oh, and Merry Christmas!"

Kate, though not particularly religious, had in fact suggested they resurrect the Mackenzie Christmas morning Mass tradition.

She'd done it partly because she was feeling nostalgic, partly because she liked the songs and ceremonies of churchy Christmas.

She'd originally had visions of dressing herself up in holiday style, but Kate found herself under the gun time-wise and traded fashion for not irritating her father. She wound up seven minutes later in the backseat of the car, half-awake in jeans and the sweatshirt she'd been sleeping in.

"Well, dear, the Lord will just be glad you are there," said her mother as she slid into the passenger seat looking infuriatingly perfect and alert. "But do keep your coat buttoned up," she added, staring at her daughter through the rearview mirror.

They arrived to find the streets around the church filled up with the cars of fair-weather Christians who turned up twice a year, apparently solely to raise Robert Mackenzie's blood pressure. "I knew we should have left earlier," he mumbled, driving wider and wider circles on the surrounding streets before finding a place to park. As the family emerged, the cold air hit Kate full in the face, making her eyes water and her nose run. She realized she had left her bag in the car but was afraid that asking her father to unlock the doors at this point might push him down the path to heart failure. Instead, she sniffed hard, trying to force the salty-slickness back up into her nostril, but it didn't work, forcing her to run her mittened hand as gently as she could across her face to try and contain it, the rough wool scratching at the chafed skin.

"This is why men always have a handkerchief with them," Robert Mackenzie said in response to Kate's plight and her sister's declaration that it was "disgusting".

"When did the station wagon become a time machine, because I don't remember being transported back to 1947," Tracy said, laughing at the statement.

"Well then, can I borrow yours, Dad? I'm having an issue here," she asked.

Deciding that she had suffered enough to learn her lesson, he handed it over, a plain white cotton square with his initials artfully stitched on one corner in a deep royal blue. It felt like satin against her face, and she took a deep breath in through her mouth so as to fully enjoy the relief to come, a satisfaction second only to scratching an itch.

Breathing again and no longer self-conscious, Kate actually smiled for the first time that morning as she handed back the crinkled square, which her father put in his coat pocket.

They were not a particularly demonstrative family,

and they weren't big talkers. They went through life precisely ticking off the events that families experience: births, deaths, holidays and graduations. They followed all protocols and rituals and traditions. They were pretty good at being a family, pretty efficient. But it was only in odd moments like these that Kate could see through the politeness and reserve to the fact that they *were* family, closer to each other than to anyone else in the world. They were the people she could give her snotty tissues to.

She wanted to tell her father that she loved him. It wasn't like the words had never been spoken between them. But looking up at him, she just couldn't quite manage to get them out, not here in the middle of the street at nine o'clock on Christmas morning. Not without the benefit of decoration, or background noise, or a drink in hand. It would sound so loud, cracking against the crisp air. Or worse, not loud enough, swallowed up by the cold, requiring him to ask her to repeat herself, embarrassing them both. So instead she just said, "Thanks, Dad," touching his forearm with her unsullied mitt and hoping he understood.

January

The New Year had not begun well. Kate had come back sad and alone from Christmas with her parents. The excitement of her career switch had been dulled by having to explain to a myriad of relatives and old friends why anyone would give up a career in a dignified profession like accounting to become someone's secretary. Especially someone in her situation, a single woman who should be stockpiling all the money she could to prepare for those long, lonely years she was sure to have. Any sense of freedom she had initially felt because of her regained singledom had been much tempered by too many nights spent wandering her apartment making busy work and trying to convince herself that she was an exciting person leading a life choc-a-block with important responsibilities. Though even sitting home alone was better than the dreadful alternative. As much as she might have hated rearranging her photo albums or eating snacks she'd made just to kill twenty minutes of an evening, it was still better than having to stick her toe back in the dating pool. She had done that enough in the past few months to know that it was a dank and frigid place, full of false hope and bravado and the embarrassment of pretending that you are not waiting by the phone for a call from a guy you'd actually thought was a dick. A place where you were to be outraged if a man paid for everything and humiliated if he didn't. A place full of creepy lighting and "it" music that no one would remember in two years and where the clothes, the rituals and the conversation seemed always to be short and uncomfortable.

It made her furious to think that one of the key motivating factors in finally telling Scott it was over had been this bizarre fantasy she had concocted of her and Megan sitting on bar stools sipping neon-coloured drinks and waiting expectantly for the approaching wave of eligible men they would spend the evening entertaining with stories about past crazy exploits.

She couldn't say she regretted leaving Scott. Just because she hadn't found someone better suited to her didn't make him a good fit. It was more that she'd been so naïvely dreaming about this sweet single life she'd have once the leash was off. How had she forgotten all about dating? The absurdity of letting a strange person touch your special bits while you attempted to smoulder and not laugh when his breath tickled your ear or his leather pants made fart noises as they rubbed against the vinyl diner bench he used for a couch.

And worse, she'd forgotten about the (majority of the) times she had dressed herself up in her best outfit —one she might have bought just for that one night, that random Thursday night—and made her face up just so and put herself out there just to be seen. Just for someone to look your way and think you were worth the price of a pint. Those neverending evenings spent sitting alone at a table with the friends you came with, an island in a sea of people all looking for someone to get ahold of for a while and yet unwilling or unable to land.

Even though she was sitting there with the people she liked most, it wasn't going to be good enough to have warranted her efforts, even though it should be. That's what people say to each other the whole time they are sitting there willing themselves to stay put and not send chairs flying across the room, jump up, cut their losses and run home to throw their individual covers over their lonely heads.

She would now think with shame about the many, many times she had told her best friend how lucky she was to be free, single and able to just pick up with any guy she wanted to. Told her sister how envious she was that Tracy got to retreat back to her own place every night and have a chance to be "alone with her thoughts". Who the fuck would want to be alone with their thoughts? That was the recipe for being totally miserable.

Oh, dating was dirty business. But even though she hated it, Kate did truly believe it was the necessary means to an end. Finding that better half. Someone to fill in the missing bits that Scott had left in her life. As much as Kate wanted transformation and wanted to bring her imagined best self out for the world to see, she hadn't emerged a butterfly from the last few months. She hadn't managed to become the whole, unique person she thought she could and should be. For all of her efforts, she'd managed to create diversions, not change. As Christmas had so painfully shown her, she hadn't matured into the kind of person people thought was better off on her own. What was worse, Kate couldn't honestly say now that she believed anyone was the kind of person who was happier alone. While it may be true that alone is sometimes preferable to the next best offer, she was certain that didn't make it the natural order of things. And Kate was a girl who longed for the natural order of things.

Which is why, when she walked into the party Tracy was throwing to ring in the New Year and saw a man dressed in all-over black give her a long, hard stare, Kate decided to stare back. And when he came to hover in her general vicinity, she turned to him and offered to get him a drink. Many drinks later, it was the same reason she decided to bring him back to her place.

It hadn't been as easy as it sounded later, even with the drinks. That was the trick of it. To hear people talk about it, the city was full of suave socialites, naturally glib gadabouts born for these kind of "pick 'em up and roll 'em over" exchanges. But Kate had to fight every natural instinct to get the job done. Every tendency towards decorum suppressed, every modest twitch or downcast gaze quickly abandoned, every realization of how totally ridiculous it was to grab a strange man's crotch and give it a squeeze while talking about the kind of music his band played set aside to haunt her another day.

Though it was unlike her to be so forward, she couldn't say that she hated it entirely. What made her uncomfortable also made her powerful. Heady stuff to realize that, while you may not be able to become a whole new person, to act like a whole new person was pretty easy. It was easier than most people imagine, than Kate herself could have imagined, to take off your panties in a taxi cab or pull a man through your bedroom door by his skinny tie just like they do in those adult Romcom shows she'd become addicted to. To leave the lights on.

That was all so easy. What was hard, Kate had discovered was trying not to regret all of those actions a half hour later, when she didn't want to be a brazen bad girl any more and wasn't sure how to tell that to the strange man lying on her bed in a post-fellatio haze, grinning at her like he was the one who had accomplished something. And it seemed she would have to tell him, since this man wasn't making any attempt to get up or out.

Try as she might not to, Kate did regret it. It wasn't a moral issue she was dealing with; she wasn't tormented by any sense of guilt or shame. It was just that it was such a fucking waste of time. Who the hell was this guy she'd just spent all of this energy on? Who she'd spent the evening performing for? He wasn't about to be Mr. Kate Mackenzie. He was just some guy. And now he was sitting there, waiting for the second act, when he hadn't deserved the first, and she just really wanted him to go.

There was a part of her that felt the polite thing to do was first to gargle, then pretend to come, then pretend to sleep, counting the minutes until she could slap on the coffee maker, hand him a cup and tell him all about the brunch she was terribly late for. But since Kate had yet to follow her inner compass that evening, she felt it was a little late to start now, so instead she decided to cap the evening's show with a plot twist and a climax of a different kind. She grinned at her guest then, wiping her mouth with her hand, she gave him a wink and headed up to give him a kiss, watching the look on his face turn from bliss to horror as he tried to push himself right through the headboard.

"Whoa, hey, what are you doing?"

"Oh, just thought I'd like another kiss," she said sweetly, placing a hand on his chest, which slipped as he managed to sit himself up.

"Oh. Cool, cool. Ummm, but aren't you thirsty? I'm really thirsty. Don't you want something to drink? Got some like, orange juice or something?"

Kate stopped advancing and sat up herself. It'd be over soon. "Sorry, I don't think I have any orange juice."

"Oh, that's okay. I can get some on my way home. I should probably be heading that way anyway. It's getting late."

"Oh, you're not going to stay?"

"Uh, no. No. I've got to be up early tomorrow."

"Oh," Kate said, sitting back on her heels and trying to look a bit disappointed. "Why? Do you have a brunch or something?" she asked innocently.

"Ummm. Yeah! Yes. Brunch. Can't get out of it, or else I'd stay," he said, hopping off the bed and zipping up his pants, seizing on her suggestion like a life raft. "So sorry. Gotta jet. But you're an awesome girl. I'd totally love to see you again. I'll call, okay?"

"Okay," Kate said, waiting long enough for him to have actually left the room before calling, "Would you like my number? So, you know, you can call me?" She reached for a pen from the bedside table. She didn't know why she was prolonging what was so obviously going nowhere, but she just couldn't help herself. At least it would give Tracy a laugh when she called for her report in the morning.

His head popped back in the door. "Oh. Yeah. Totally. What's your number?"

She walked over to him and wrote it on his hand, then walked with him to the front door, watching the wheels turning behind his eyes as he tried to figure out the best way to say goodbye to her without getting anywhere near her mouth. It was hilarious and tragic, and she could feel herself getting giddy. She was tempted to ask him why, if he was so repulsed by the idea of his own semen, he had been so willing to let her have a shot of it, but of course she didn't. People never said those things they always wished they could say.

But she debated telling Tracy that she'd asked him that as he kissed the top of her head, telling her he'd call her soon.

It is fair to say that Kate was not only surprised, but stunned when, in fact, he did call her. Three days later. She was so stunned in fact that she actually agreed to go out with him when he said he was in the neighbourhood and wondered if she didn't have that evening free.

"What did you have in mind?" she asked him, putting her finger to her lips, a warning to Tracy and Megan, since she'd set the call to speakerphone when she'd seen his name come up on the call display.

"Well, I'd tell you, but I'd have to kill you," he said. Kate watched Tracy fall to the floor and roll around with the agony of suppressing her laughter, but somewhere deep inside her, Kate felt a little spark ignite.

"Well then, I guess I'll have to wait and find out." She knew she sounded cutesy and tried not to look at the mock resuscitation Megan was now performing on her sister.

"Not that long, I can be at your place in fifteen minutes. Can you be ready then?"

"Oh, yeah sure, see you then? You know where it is?"

"Oh, yeah, I remember the building with the Beer Store in the bottom."

"Right," Kate smiled. Men always remembered that. She was about to tell him her buzzer number when he surprised her by asking, "Is your last name on the buzzer list?" It wasn't really much to be impressed by, but Kate would take what she could get.

"Yep."

"Cool." A pause.

"It's Mackenzie," she said quietly, but not quite quietly enough, and her sister let out a snort of laughter that echoed in the room.

"'kay, see you," Kate called, dropping the receiver and glaring at the other two. "You assholes."

"What?" Megan said, wiping the tears from her eyes. "Are you kidding?" Catching the look on Kate's face, she sniffed. "You're the one that put him on speakerphone. And anyway, you said he was an idiot."

"Yeah, well, he is. But he's nice," Kate said lamely. She was agitated. He was *not* nice. And she didn't like him. Fact was, he was there, and miracle of miracles, he was different. Or at least, *this* was different. This hadn't happened to her before. Not just that he was a one-night stand coming back, but that he'd even asked her out on a genuine date at a set time.

Kate was not often asked out on dates. She was regularly stopped and asked for directions, but never for dates. Any relationship she'd had was built on inference and things left unsaid:

"My friends will be hanging out at Max's tonight."

"I'm playing a show at the ElMo on Friday."

"Have you seen that new German art house flick? Looks good."

Never had anyone called and said "Are you free now, because I would like to take you out on a date." She was flattered. She couldn't help it. And it wasn't just a date, but an adventure. Where was she going? Who knew? Somewhere mysterious, with a guy who played in a band. It could be anything, a show, a gallery opening, she had no idea what would happen.

She had no idea what to wear.

"Oh hell, oh hell, oh hell. What am I going to wear?"

"Not that," said Tracy pointing at the sweatpants and polar fleece robe Kate had on.

"Don't be a bitch right now, and please help me find a shirt or something."

"Seriously, I thought you didn't like the guy?" said Megan, trying not to feel put out that their movie night was obviously cancelled.

"I know, it's just…"

"Better than nothing is just that. I get it," said Tracy. When she went into protective big sister mode, she did it very well. "What kind of shirt?" she said, following Kate's trail of fuzzy slippers and hair elastics down the hallway and into the bedroom with Megan hot, if sullen, on her heels.

"I dunno. A fun shirt. An 'I'm a madcap girl on an adventure' shirt," Kate said, spraying toothpaste on the mirror while she sprayed perfume in her armpits, unable to find her deodorant. She'd just recently shaved. It wasn't a good idea.

Wincing, she walked through the ensuite into her bedroom. "Did you find anything? He's going to be here any minute."

Tracy held up a black tank top. "You should wear this with your 'ass' pants," she said, turning as Kate dropped her bathrobe. "And a bra," she added, staring at her sister's breasts. "Hey. Did you know your nipples are crooked?"

"What are 'ass' pants?" asked Megan.

"My nipples are crooked?" asked Kate.

"Those jeans she bought last summer. They make her ass look smaller."

"Would you fuck off about my imperfections," Kate pleaded, yanking the shirt out of Tracy's hands and slipping it over her head while Megan fished out the jeans and a black cashmere sweater.

"You'll need this too."

"Now, *you* I like," Kate replied, sliding on the rest of the outfit and sitting down on the floor to wrangle on a pair of boots. She ran a hand through her hair and looked up at the other two with a look of childish expectation. "Where do you think we are going to go?"

"Honey, don't get your hopes up too high," Megan said cautiously, softening it as Kate looked away. "No, I'm not being a bitch, I just mean…oh, it'll be great, I'm sure, but probably dinner or something."

"The dude's a loose cannon. I figure if she doesn't end up with her head in a freezer, she can safely call it a success," said Tracy with a laugh. Kate smiled, but the lips were thin. "C'mon, Katie, I was just kidding."

"I know. I know," Kate said, taking a deep breath to calm her nerves before explaining. "I just want it to be something nice. That's all."

There was a knock at the door that stopped them from responding, but they both held out a hand to help Kate to her feet.

"I'll get it," said Tracy.

"No, you damn well won't. You two stay in here," Kate hissed, heading down the hall and listening for the inevitable footsteps thumping behind her. She drew one more calming breath while she waited for them to arrange themselves in the living room and opened the door.

He was standing there, a tulip in hand and dressed again in head-to-toe black. Perfect.

"I walked in behind some old lady," he said, leaning in to kiss her on the cheek. Less perfect, but still okay.

"So much for building security," Megan whispered, still not entirely over being dumped by her best friend for some idiot man. Tracy snorted appreciatively, hoping to head off any further outbursts. She thought the guy was an idiot too, knew it from her own experience. But she would have done the same thing. Kate looked over at them pleadingly, making Megan feel bad enough to slap on a smile as Kate said, "This is Megan, and Tracy you know." She waved in their general direction.

"Oh. Hey," he said, opting not to introduce himself to Megan, then turning his attention to Kate, smiling as he asked her, "How about you and me grab a coffee?"

Kate felt a bit like she'd walked into a patio door, repeating "Coffee?" louder than she meant to.

His smile dimmed a little. "Um, yeah. I have a rehearsal in the neighbourhood and thought we could grab a coffee before I head over."

Kate wondered if there was any worse feeling in the world than feeling like a fool.

"Oh. Great! Coffee!" she said, the words coming out in staccato bursts. She felt her throat closing as she swallowed back tears. She turned and looked into four sympathetic eyes saying, "Okay girls, I'm heading off to Starbucks. Don't wait up." Then, unable to look at them any more, she grabbed her purse and sailed toward the elevator.

"She told me she likes coffee," he said stupidly to Tracy before shutting the door behind him.

"Oh, poor Katie," said Megan.

"Poor Tim, more like."

"Are you kidding me? Did you see the size of the nostrils on that guy? She'd better not get him too excited. If he started heavy breathing, I bet he could vacuum with those things."

Tracy laughed before turning to the mirror on the wall and flipping up her top. "Mine are even, aren't they?"

*　*　*

Tim, sensing something was amiss with his coffee plans, suggested that maybe he and Katie could go for a drink instead. She agreed, settling down noticeably, so they headed to a chain-pub located on the corner, one of the ones that seem to be on every corner, right beside the Starbucks.

He ordered two pints for them and paid, to Katie's delight, which was short-lived, since he turned to inform her that she could get the next round. This she did soon thereafter, nerves and the stark realization that they had absolutely nothing to say to each other having made them abnormally thirsty. Kate was not a huge drinker, but she wasn't too drunk after her second drink. Just drunk enough to think that ordering a third one would be a good idea. It was not. The third was enough for Tim to decide that practice wasn't that important, and the fourth round went by in a blur. Before her fifth Kate remembered waltzing over to the ATM machine, having run through her emergency cheap date money and figuring they'd be there for a while.

They were not. Three sips into what was to be her last drink of the evening, in the minutes after she'd just remarked on how she didn't feel even a little bit drunk and just after she'd hit send on a text to her best friend and sister telling them to evacuate the premises as there was going to be some good lovin' tonight, Katie got an awful feeling. One awfully familiar to her. Then she tilted her head to the side of the table, and daintily as she could, threw up forty dollars worth of a local microbreweries' finest all over the hardwood floor. She remembered bits of what happened next. Throwing up again in the bushes outside the pub. Asking Tim to wait with her while she sat a minute in the street. Telling him he'd probably be nicer if he was a Jamie as he propped her up in the elevator. And finally, painfully, she remembered him bringing her into her bedroom, where she got on her knees and, feeling dehydrated, took a little sip out of her cat's water dish. She remembered giving him the stink eye when he told her that was disgusting and telling him that he wasn't very rock and roll. And finally, she remembered lifting her face off of the carpet to see his shoes heading for the door. This was where she woke up a few hours later with a throbbing head, swollen tongue and a powerful urge to throw up again.

She crawled into the bathroom and sat by the toilet a good long while, feeling the cool porcelain against her cheek as she ignored the persistent ring of the telephone. While she sat there, she thought up a poem that she proceeded to write down on a roll of toilet paper with an old eyeliner pencil that had fallen under the sink.

Love can make your head spin. You know what else can make your head spin? A Hangover.
Love can last a lifetime. A Hangover can, apparently, last an entire day.
Love will leave you exhausted and disoriented.
A hangover, ditto.
I'd prefer love.

She thought they might be the lyrics to a song, and she'd pass them on to Tim if she ever heard from him again.

She didn't hear from him again. If she had, she would have been humiliated. The fact that he didn't call didn't break her heart (Megan had been right about the nostrils), but it did chip it a little, all the same.

It was so strange, she knew, to miss him. She'd hardly even known who he was. The total hours she'd spent alone with him equaled less than some hair appointments she'd had, and she'd been drunk for almost all of those hours. But she missed him just the same.

He'd been a moment in what had been a long and

predictable time since her split with Scott. He was a change, a possibility of change. An inlet in the river of her everyday happenings: the morning espressos and nine-to-fives and TV movies and after dinner drinks.

It wasn't that time stood still or any other horrendous notion like that. It was more that for a little bit of time, she'd felt chosen. She was the one that had been picked. When she'd seen him at the party, she'd felt lucky. From the minute she'd seen him watching her, the game was on. It had been so unlike her to gaze at someone, inching them forward with an arch of her eyebrow. So unusual to laugh easily with someone strange to her and to bring him home that night.

And when he'd called her, it had been so unlikely, so out of the blue. She felt like she'd somehow beaten the odds. She felt beyond flattered, almost blessed.

That's why, the day after the date, when she'd finally dressed herself and drunk some strong coffee and invited Megan over to turn ugly personal tragedy into funny dating lore, she'd kept one ear cocked slightly towards the living room phone.

The next day she went back to work, cursing herself for the calls she made home to check for a message she was certain would not arrive and honestly didn't want.

The day after that, she called her mother, knowing there was no need to keep the line free. She poured herself a glass of wine and flicked on the television.

One more day, and she told her sister she was up for a drink on the way home from the office.

And the next day she missed him.

February

HTTP—"Dammit," Glynniss muttered, searching for the delete key on her hand-me-down computer. It was an oldie Stuart had given her when it no longer suited his working needs. She didn't use it much. She turned it on occasionally just to clear out the endless forwarded jokes and recipes she received from her sister. Helen couldn't get enough of rhinos humping each other and "You Know You Are a Child of the 60s" compilation lists.

Aside from that, Glynniss hardly went near it. Stuart had set her up with some fancy super-speed connection that she was now forced to pay fifty good dollars each month for. Some gift.

She found computers about as intuitive as men. Everything had to be spelled out perfectly, each little slash and dash and colon in its place. It was infuriating, even though she was, had been, a very good typist.

But she was determined to master the machine on this particular evening, driven by a higher power—love. It was February now. Almost six months since Emily had broken Stuart's heart, and Glynniss had decided six months was time enough for mending. She had a plan to find Stuart a woman. Someone to make him laugh and take care of him and give him babies, or at the very least a reason to get a haircut and start shaving regularly again.

She'd been riding home on the subway from a visit to her aunt's when the idea first came to her. Feeling full and lethargic after a decent dinner and a stiff sherry, she had been in no mood for the historical biography she was lugging around in her purse. Glyniss never travelled without her book, a shield against the weird men and crying babies so fond of public transit. That night she sat, her head resting on the Plexiglas guard, too tired to care about the million germs probably crawling into her ear, and stared blindly at the advertisements lining the subway car, until one came into focus. It was a caricature of a man, tall and cartoon-y, with sharp features and a mop of brown hair. He looked to her like Stuart. He was sitting on a bench gazing happily at a blonde cartoon counterpart with a big smile and bigger chest. Below them in large white letters was a website address: www.thesingle-solution.com.

Staring at it, Glyniss read the line, dreamily sounding out plausible syllables until the light dawned: "The Single Solution." It was a dating site. One of several screaming for the attention of the city's lonely masses these days. She'd heard about them on the radio and seen the happy couples on television. She had always thought them a bit of a scam.

No. Not so much a scam. They weren't seedy. Shabby was the better word. You couldn't just go ordering up a lover like it was a book or cosmetic set, she'd told herself.

But sitting there, lulled by the swaying of the train

and the simple happiness promised in the ad, Glyniss asked herself, why the hell not? While she didn't pull the pen out of her purse to jot the address down, she did slowly repeat it to herself for the remainder of her trip.

It was sometime the next evening, as she sat with a cup of tea on the couch Stuart had occupied for most of the fall, that it popped back into her head. Stuart had managed to find himself a decent space to call his own, due in large part to Graham, which Glyniss had not quite forgiven him for. So now they were both alone. She was so used to it that she didn't really miss his company, having long ago found practical ways to fill her hours. She missed being needed, of course, but she managed quite nicely.

Her son she wasn't so sure about. Stuart had never actually been on his own before, having jumped from his mother's house to residence at school to shared apartments of varying sizes and states of disrepair, finally into Emily's apartment. Though he was an introvert, not much of a joiner, Stuart really was the kind of boy better off around other people. He was someone who needed taking care of and who people naturally wanted to nurture. He had never had to figure out how well he'd do when the person taking care of him was Stuart.

Glyniss wasn't sure now was the best time for such an experiment. He said he was doing fine in the new place, enjoying the freedom and all of that blather; playing at being a grown-up. But he wasn't getting any younger, and now was the time he should be putting forth his best effort to get a girl who was still worth getting. Glyniss knew he hadn't made any attempt to find such a person on his own. If she could no longer be the one who was going to take care of him, maybe her role was to find him someone who could.

She held her mug up close to her face, breathing in the hot steam, eyes closed, and tried to visualize the ad she'd stared at last evening, hoping to recall the name of the dating site. She could see the animated Stuart, the girl, the sparkly winter scenery. Her eyes snapped open. She had it; The Single Solution. She didn't move right away, her mind still circling around whether or not this was a good idea. Stuart wouldn't like it, but a mother, even one as unsure of herself as Glyniss, knows that sometimes you have to be unliked to get the job done. Nodding with satisfaction, she stood up and walked the short distance over to her desk. It couldn't hurt to have a look.

She pressed the power button on the computer, jumping a little as it chimed to life. There she now sat, typing erroneous characters into the search bar of the browser.

Taking her time, she tapped away her last bad start and slowly, carefully tried it again, this time with success.

A vivid red page filled with heart-shaped graphics and beautiful anime faces popped up on screen. Well, she was on the right site.

Now what? Glyniss thought to herself, scanning the page, drinking in all of the information, and searching for some clue as to what she was supposed to do next. Her eyes stopped at the words "Free Trial". She waited until the arrow became a finger, just like Stuart had taught her to, pressed the mouse button, pleased to see the screen changing in response.

Free was what she wanted. She didn't know much about the Internet, but she knew better than to go signing up for things you had to pay for. She was well aware that she might as well just offer her entire identity up for sale on "the eBay" if she were going to go around typing her personal information into websites. She was loathe even to use the gift cards Graham and Jane had given her for Christmas to buy books online. Every time a book she ordered showed up at her door, she considered it something of a miracle.

So free trial it was. She was then prompted to select the kind of "sexy single" she wanted to meet. This was a pause for thought. It's very rare that a mother, at least a mother like Glyniss, is allowed any say in the kind of girl who will have the honour of dating her son. A pity, but Glyniss had never really given tons of thought to what sort of girl would suit him best. There were so many factors.

If she was too quiet, Stuart might sink further into himself. Too outgoing and he'd be overshadowed. A professional might make him feel emasculated, but someone without a career might make him feel overburdened in the money department. If she was too clingy, Glyniss would never see him; too independent and she'd up and leave him one day when he was at the store. She had no idea where to start and was glad to see that The Single Solution had accounted for such questions and others she hadn't even considered. The site offered a variety of personality quizzes with ingenious names like: "Similar Traits Make for Happy Mates" and "Let the Zodiac Help You Bring the Love Back".

She absently took a sip of her tea and began selecting radio buttons until the love doctors had made it clear Stuart's life would be made complete by a Sagittarius who was into music, children and Thai food, and who was woman enough to let her man be a man. Armed with this knowledge, Glyniss turned her attention to Step Two, eyeing three drop down menus designed to help you search out the person of your dreams from the "over 15,000 sexy singles just waiting to meet you!"

She made quick work of her options.

Sex: Female.

Age: 25 to 35.

Any younger, and they'd be foolish, any older and they'd be desperate.

Relationship:

Hmm… this was a tricky one. The options included long-term relationship (sounded a little heavy to know about on the first date); one-nighter (indecent and bound to end in a trip to the clinic). The only other option was casual dating, and Glyniss knew what that meant to Stuart and his friends. Dating as many people as you can get your hands on, literally. Long-term relationship it was.

Having selected the last of her options, Glyniss hit the "Surrender Your Singledom!" button and watched the screen flood with women. And that was just the first screen—there were pages of them.

A quick scan showed most of these women considered themselves to be so fit and fun that they "couldn't believe they were actually using a dating site".

How was a person supposed to choose one girl out

of all of these apologetic women, she thought? It was awful. Parading yourself out there amongst all the other "super friendly" women, vowing that they loved watching sports and promising they weighed ten pounds less than they actually did. They didn't have any self-respect. Here they were putting out a casting call for spouses. How many men would be caught doing that?

Pushing the "back" button on the browser, Glyniss decided to find out. She reached the search page, entering new options.

Sex: Male.

Age:

She'd intended to select the same age range from the menu but then saw a selection marked "60+" she hadn't noticed in the women's option. Probably because an older woman knew better than to go begging love from total strangers. Her mouse travelled down along the screen, highlighting the words. 60+. Horndogs, she thought, but her finger pressed down on the button. She was curious. It'd be a laugh.

Relationship:

Oh, one-nighter, definitely. Double horndogs. She submitted her request then snorted with laughter as the page popped up, an ad promising to cure erectile dysfunction swimming lazily across the top. Good place for it, she thought, looking at the dozens of mini profiles her search had returned; dozens of poster boys for seniors' homes, all selling their "vast life experience" and looking for thirty-year-olds to share it with.

Glyniss snorted again, reaching for her cup and taking a swallow of tea, now tepid and unappetizing.

She decided she'd pour herself a nice little glass of liquor instead, then get back to business. There had to be at least one good woman for her boy in the thousands here. Not everyone who came to the site had to be a sicko. She sat back down, preparing for an hour of serious daughter-in-law shopping. But there was one more thing she wanted to see, just for fun. She changed her last search parameters to long-term relationship and submitted her request once again. She felt her face flush a little as she did it and took another sip from her glass, hoping to blame it on that.

More faces. More grandpas. But this time the write-ups were different. "I'm a widower", "I would like someone to go to movies with", "I've moved to be near my grandkids and I'm looking for company", that sort of thing.

They weren't at all funny. Some of them were even a bit sad, and Glyniss was drawn in by these mini-histories. These were people who weren't horny, or greedy, or deluded. They were photos of people who were lonely. These were testimonials to the labours of people actively trying not to be lonely. She stared at the lined and wrinkled faces genuinely open to the possibility of second, maybe third chances. Some were even brave or foolish enough to say that they were looking for True Love. At their age. Her age. It was utterly ridiculous, but now Glyniss wasn't laughing. In fact, she thought that maybe she might cry, staring into the eyes of these friendly, average-looking men. Nice-looking men. With grandkids and antique cars and vegetable gardens they tended themselves.

She forgot to feel like a voyeur as she continued

scanning the profiles. She was fascinated because, to be honest, Glyniss didn't really know any men. Her sons yes, to some degree. Helen's husband and a nephew and nephew-in-law, her doctor, if that counted. But since she'd retired, there had been very little non-familial contact with men of any kind. After a certain age, where would she have gone to see them? She wasn't much of a joiner either, and any activity she did in the community was at the behest of her aunt and usually involved a group of white-haired ladies.

She certainly didn't know any men in an intimate way; again, she didn't think her doctor counted. Though she never said it, even to herself, she hadn't known a man that way since her husband had left her, decades ago.

Since she hadn't thought about it, she hadn't really thought about the fact that she would probably never be intimate with anyone ever again. She'd had her share of intimacy, and she wasn't to be granted any more.

It wasn't just sex. Sex had never been as pleasant for Glyniss as she thought it ought to be. She had always been too wrapped up in the desire to remain dignified while lying on her back with her knees beside her ears to really get into the spirit of things.

It was intimacy these men were asking her to consider. She had never stopped to think about the fact that no one was going to drum their fingers lightly on the small of her back ever again, or grab hold of her knee while she sat in the passenger seat of a car.

No one was ever going to slow down to wait for her while she stopped to look in a store window or absently reach for her hand in the grocery store parking lot.

None of it would ever happen for her again. She'd

known it, she supposed, the way she knew she was going to die one day, and that she was never really going to sign up to take that historical writing course at the university she kept telling people she was interested in. She knew it, but she didn't think about it. What was the point? The truth was that while she might not like it, there wasn't anything to be done about it.

Except, here was a collection of people who had all thought about it, who had found it unacceptable, and had decided there was something to be done about it. Now she was thinking about it too, and it was all a little overwhelming.

The phone rang, causing Glyniss to jump and spill her drink.

"Yes?" she said angrily, wiping up the sticky puddle with the sleeve of her bathrobe, turning the white velour a mottled and sickly shade of green.

"Hey." It was Helen. "What's up with you?"

"Nothing, why?"

"You just sound a bit short, that's all. Did I catch you at a bad time?"

"Nothing," Glyniss stammered. "I mean, no. I'm not doing anything," she said, turning off the monitor to prove herself correct. "I was in bed."

"Oh ho, spending a little quality time with yourself, huh?" Helen chuckled, satisfied that she'd discovered the reason for her sister's distracted air.

"That's not funny! Don't be such a sicko, Helen. I was simply going to sleep," Glyniss choked, blushing scarlet, and worried that she'd cry now for certain.

"Oh well, then sorry to bother," Helen sniffed, offended. "Call me tomorrow when you've had some

rest and located your sense of humour, will you?"
Helen was always making light. Everything was
funny, even her own cancer. Helen would eat her alive
if she ever got wind of anything she had been doing or
thinking about that night. The solution wasn't to get
Helen to stop laughing, as Agathe liked to say, it was for
Glyniss to stop caring that she laughed. But Glyniss
would always care.

The line went dead in her ear. She hung up the
receiver and reached for the monitor button but
hesitated. She looked at the mess she'd made of her
desk and her clothes, and she found herself tired and
desperate for bed. She stood and removed her robe,
throwing it over the soggy papers and stained lace cloth
on the desk. Then she bent and unplugged the
computer from the wall before heading to bed.

In the morning, she removed the whole mess, robe
and all, with a swipe of her arm and carried it down
the hall to the garbage chute.

She plugged in the computer, starting her morning
coffee as it reloaded itself. She turned on her browser,
found the history panel and erased it. She wouldn't be
going back. Glyniss was not one of the people who
could go shopping for love. Stuart would have to find a
woman himself.

*   *   *

Once a year, Jennifer Davies made a public nod to
social justice by renting ice time at a local hockey rink
and hosting a charity skating party that brought
together an awkward mix of underprivileged kids and

overcompensated lawyers with guilt complexes. It was second only to the Davies and Associates Christmas parties on the list of events Stuart refused to miss. There were ridiculous liability waivers to sign and excruciating conversations to overhear as he circled the ice, one hand skimming the boards, the other holding a cup of spiked hot chocolate.

"Do you have any brothers or sisters, Jimmy?"

"My brother's in jail."

"Oh. Well that's...okay."

This year, to make the whole thing even more deliciously awful, Jennifer had booked the ice on February fourteenth, and the arena was awash in shiny red hearts and hair metal love songs. Nothing makes a harassment lawyer more uncomfortable when holding the hand of an unknown minor than holding that hand while listening to the musical stylings of David Coverdale.

Stuart was thrilled to be doing something so over the top on Cupid's big day. He had been secretly worried he would have some issues with Valentine's Day as a single guy. He was afraid he'd end up drunk and alone, whispering sweet nothings into Emily's answering machine. He hadn't called her in months, not since he'd found out she'd become engaged over the holidays, aware that he couldn't fit one more nail in that particular coffin. But these fabricated holidays could do strange things to a romantic like Stuart, who had been spending increasing amounts of time on his own.

He'd made the unfortunate mistake of replacing most of his friends with Emily's in the years they dated, and now with Elizabeth so inconveniently married, he found himself sadly lacking company. There were the guys he could call and have a drink with now and again, but he didn't really know them any more, so they'd spend most of their time together reminiscing about university and quoting lines from an impressive range of television shows. Sometimes a night like that was fun, but he couldn't make a habit of those evenings, because it made him start to feel like all his friends were kind of stupid. Worse was the eventual realization that he didn't have a single person with whom he could have a conversation about people that existed in the real world (not the *Real World*). This would then make him realize he was kind of stupid too.

More and more, he had been spending his winter days and nights in front of one glowing screen or another. In an attempt to get himself out of the house, he had in the past few weeks been taking the training sessions needed to volunteer at a local distress hotline he'd read about on one local blog or another. He had thought that hearing about other people's crappy lives might give him a little perspective on his own. But he sure as hell didn't want to be hanging out there on Valentine's Day. No, he'd give his time and charity on that particular day to disadvantaged kids and uncoordinated lawyers on skates.

Elizabeth was surprisingly willing to have him tag along, even though it did sort of reinforce all of the rumours that had been circling her office since they had shown up together at the Christmas party. But she had been a little concerned about Stuart's decision to get involved with a trauma hotline and thought that volunteering with kids was a much more suitable way to do some good in the world and to achieve the end goal of removing his head from his ass.

Plus, Michael was spending the weekend locked up in his study preparing for court on Monday, and she needed someone to skate pledge-athon laps in her pregnant stead. Stuart's participation left her free to sip hot chocolate from the warm and cozy bar area overlooking the ice and watch as her plan to flatter Cupid in the sincerest of ways unfolded down below.

Stuart was making his inaugural lap when he saw her, the young blonde woman clinging nervously to the boards as she stepped onto the ice. She looked vaguely familiar, and he figured it was because he probably remembered her from the Christmas party.

Something about the way she looked, hands spread in front of her, pigtails sticking out from a black toque, made him think he should go over and see if she needed a hand.

She looked easy. Not in a sexual way, more in the way that made Stuart think he could actually say a few words to her and not be shot down on site. She looked nice.

Watching him slide across the ice, tucking his hands into the pockets of his jeans like a little kid, Elizabeth smiled with satisfaction, leaning towards the lawyer sitting a few chairs over.

"I knew it! Halfway there, wouldn't you say?"

The other woman followed Elizabeth's finger and saw Kate giving a tall guy in jeans and wool cable knit sweater a once-over, with a blush creeping into her cheeks. She frowned.

"Isn't that your buddy?" Megan asked Elizabeth.

"Yes, it is, Stuart's the name," was the smiling reply.

"Doesn't he have a fiancée?" Megan asked, thinking back on the bits of office chatter she'd picked up after the holiday party. There were plenty to choose from, but that was the one currently bothering Megan the most.

"What? Oh, Jesus no. Not for months."

"Oh? Oh, really?" Megan said, leaning forward and thinking that Stuart was now worth a second look.

He was tall and kind of slim, but not grossly so. Good-looking, she thought, but she'd have to go down for a closer look. Kate looked pleased enough to have him standing there grabbing at her left elbow when her foot hit the board, causing her to stumble.

"Really."

"Well, in that case, can I get you another cup of cocoa? I think we might have a show to watch."

"Make mine a coffee," whispered Elizabeth, but not quietly enough to avoid a raised eyebrow from one of the receptionists from the accounting department.

"Judger," Elizabeth muttered to herself before turning her attention back to the show.

The show was, of course, horribly boring. Watching Stuart and Kate circle the ice for the umpteenth time, Megan was finally forced to commit to doing a few laps herself in the hopes of getting a little dirt. Her progress was halted when she was cornered by Jennifer on her way back to the lounge and volun-told to take a kid with abysmal skating skills and a bad personality around the ice until what seemed the end of time.

For Kate, the time was flying. She had seen Stuart at the Christmas party and had even asked Megan about him after. This was why she also thought he had a fiancée. Still, she wasn't irritated that he had come along to flirt with her. In fact, she thought it was awesome. It was amazing what a little bit of male attention could do to a girl's complexion. She was glowing, and since she thought she knew nothing could come of it, she felt quite comfortable flirting back.

He had told her his name, his occupation and that he was a huge music fan, and she told him the same. They had just finished playing a mutually successful "stump the music lover" duel that allowed both of them to show off their particular knowledge specialties of mid-to-late twentieth century contemporary music —his the country-tinged rock of the late 1970s, hers the synth-infused tunes of the alternative 1980s.

By the time their final laps were approaching, she felt so comfortable, she blurted out, "What I wouldn't give to find a guy like you. Well, minus the fiancée and the affinity for the Lynyrd Skynyrd." And she didn't even blush.

Stuart stopped skating and looked at her. She thought she heard his breath catch a bit, just in the back of his throat, before he said, "Really? A guy like me?"

"That's what I said, mister." She smiled, more than happy to let him fish for another compliment. It was such a pity that you could only flirt this well with men you couldn't have.

Stuart slowly started off again, and after a few strokes said, "Right. So you're saying that it would be fair to assume that if I didn't have a girl, you'd ask me out?"

Sure, why not, Kate thought. "Sure, why not," Kate said.

"Because I don't." His cheeks burned as he said it, just a little, but he was thankful they were skating side by side, so she couldn't look him directly in the face.

"Don't what?"

"Have a fiancée."

Now it was Kate who stopped skating, sharply enough to have them back-ended by a little guy rounding the corner behind them. Once they'd picked him up, ignoring that fact that he had called them both assholes, and sent him on his way, she said, "Yes, you do," looking at him stupidly. Then to prove her point, she added, "Megan said so."

"Well, Megan's a few months behind the times."

Kate gulped audibly. This she had not expected. All that blushing she'd been saving up came upon her cheeks at once, and it seemed combustion was imminent.

As for Stuart, he was finding it almost impossible to believe that he was about to land himself a date. Here he was talking to a pretty girl who had already said she would say yes. Best. Luck. Ever. Take the possibility of rejection out of a situation like this, and it seems not just impossible, but wrong somehow not to replace it with a little swagger.

"So here I am, all single and you on the record as interested. Ready to take me on?"

Kate was finding this situation a little cutesy. Things don't work out like this. It's too easy, she thought, it is simply too easy. She thought it best to poke around a little, looking for the downside so it didn't get the chance to take her by surprise.

"Uh…you're not heartbroken or anything, are you?"

Road block. Stuart had to think a moment to make sure he didn't turn his sure thing into a maybe. How best to answer this question? How to ride the razor-thin line between honesty, believability and pathos? "Katie," he started. Oh, he was already calling her Katie. She loved that. "Let's just say it is a little bit bruised but still ticking," Stuart told her, then felt it only polite to return the question. "How is yours? You don't have a hidden fiancé in the woodwork for me to worry about, do you?" He thought he'd successfully answered her question and lightened the mood.

"Well, actually…" Kate began as an image of Scott popped unbidden into her head.

Oh, crap. That blew, even though Stuart was pretty sure that, if she asked him out, he was going to say yes, regardless of her emotional state.

"Not a fiancé. A boyfriend. Ex-boyfriend. His name was Scott. Is Scott. He's not dead."

Dumb fuckin' luck, thought Stuart, trying not to look as defeated as he felt. He wasn't even sure what you were supposed to say to something like that. He was about to say sorry for lack of anything better, when Kate shrugged her shoulders and blurted out: "But I broke up with him. He used to keep his beer in the freezer." Which sounded as stupid to Stuart as Kate was afraid that it might, so she added, "Ummm, it was complicated."

Stuart still wasn't sure how to respond. There was a part of him that was glad to hear she'd been the dumper, and another part irrationally incensed that she would have dumped someone over something like that. If a guy can't even keep his beer in the freezer, he might as well just hand in his balls at the door. Women were so fucking hard to please.

They stared at each other for a minute until another near miss from an incoming delinquent propelled them both into the boards, and Stuart caught a whiff of the perfume Kate was wearing.

"Want to tell me about it over dinner?" he asked, eyes closed. He opened them up to see a little smile working the corners of her mouth.

"Yeah," she responded, "okay…yes."

*   *   *

So it is, two souls of a certain age, abused by love but willing to go back for more, see each other over a tottering sea of underprivileged youth and find a connection on the feast of Saint Valentine's Day. They head out of the chilly arena and into the cozy confines of a pub, where they warm themselves with a roaring fire and amber liquid and the pleasure of each other's company.

Is it love?

It is not.

"Of course it's not going to be love," said Kate a few hours later, after they had finished talking about their past hurts and current existences and future goals (or lack thereof). "Who could stand up to the pressure of all that promise? It's crushing."

"Sing it, sister," said Stuart, raising his pint glass in salute. The pair had decided, over the hours they'd spent talking easily about a myriad of other topics, that while they had all the qualities each was looking for in the other, the quantities were off. She was just a bit too into Eighties music for Stuart's taste, and while he did like the idea of one day settling outside the city, he didn't seem to like it enough for Kate. The funny thing was they didn't find it the slightest bit awkward to discuss that either. "It's too bad, though, because I think that I genuinely like you," said Stuart. Then (because you can't just look someone in the eyes and tell them you genuinely like them. The sincerity of it could make your skin crawl), he added, "And by genuinely like you, I mean I'm really sorry I'm not going to get to 'tap that ass', as the kids say."

"Oh, no worries," Kate said casually. "While there is no chance for any meaningful relationship here, I'm still totally up for having sex." She grinned in a way that caused Stuart to cough a small amount of his beer into the sleeve of his jacket, and she waited for him to recover before continuing. "Or at least, I would be if this was an episode of some smutty teen drama and not, you know…reality."

"Another reason why it would never have worked out would probably be that I hate you," he said, feeling slightly embarrassed and genuinely relieved.

Kate smiled and sat back in her chair. She hadn't expected anything good to happen that day, definitely hadn't expected to end up in a bar with a boy who thought she looked cute in her black hat and puffy jacket and laughed at her jokes. Even if he wasn't the one, even if it wasn't everything, it was all right. It was a good day.

"Happy Valentine's Day, Stuart," she said, tipping her glass towards him.

"Same to you, Katie."

March

It was seven p.m. by his watch. It had been seven p.m. for the past seven months. It wasn't as though time had stopped the day she'd broken up with him. It was just that the battery had died on that day, just about the time he was reading her letter. It was a strange coincidence, though in the history of the world, not that strange really. Not like running into the twin you'd never known about in the line-up at a grocery store or anything.

When asked why he didn't get it fixed, his standard response was that he kept forgetting. And it was true. He did forget about it, for days sometimes. Even though it was the first thing he put on each morning before even a fresh pair of boxers, he wasn't much of a watch guy. He wore it because he'd been wearing it for years, since the day his mother had given it to him at his graduation. A serious timepiece, chunky and silver. It had cost her a fortune, and he knew it. She'd bought it to show him how much she loved him, and he knew that too. It was a trait he had inherited from her. In the preceding years, it had become almost a part of him, and his wrist felt too vulnerable, too dainty to be long without it. So he wore it dead.

But the forgetting wasn't why he hadn't had it fixed.

The reason, though he'd be too ashamed to ever admit it, was that he felt, hoped perhaps, that the timing meant something. He wanted there to be some cosmic reason that the watch had died the exact(ish) moment he'd picked up that letter.

So he continued to put it on each morning, joking to anyone who noticed it had stopped that "Even a broken watch is right twice a day," a terrible line he'd heard once from his father. He secretly tried to find a little meaning in the fact that he was alone, and Emily was now married to someone else.

He'd started fixating on it in the past few months. It didn't help that Elizabeth had become so happy with Michael. Another random guy who'd basically just showed up and managed to lasso one of his women. According to these new accelerated relationship timelines, he'd been alone longer than Moses had wandered the damn desert.

He didn't think it was fair, since on his more positive days, he liked to think he'd come a pretty long way since September. It was a lot to take in, this new reality that love wasn't really what made the world go around and that life without it didn't seem much different than before. Except that he felt shitty more of the time. From his own experience, and in the many recent talks he'd had with Kate on the subject, he'd managed to wrap his head around the unpleasant fact that sometimes being with someone was the alternative to being alone, but it was not the cure for being lonely.

If you scratched his newly single surface, he hadn't really changed at all. But there was a sliver that held out, that still wanted to believe that if he was on his own, there was someone, something (the gods, the elements, the stars, what have you) that had made it so.

Stuart had never given much thought to things like astrology before the break-up. He had thought it the domain of desperate, long-nailed and hairy-armpitted women clutching crystals in one hand and a cup of tealeaves in the other. He knew he was a Leo, but that was about it.

In trying to find meaning in his busted watch, he'd googled the significance of the number seven, bringing up pages worth of numerology sites, which he began to read with an increasing interest that became stranger and more urgent as time went on. As it turned out, the number seven actually meant something, any number of things depending on which link you clicked. He became enchanted with the number seven and its prime importance in the world.

Why were there seven days in the week?

Why Seven Wonders of the World?

Why seven deadly sins?

Why seven dwarves?

The questions were endless and the answers contradictory but plentiful. And Stuart was looking for answers.

He became so fascinated by it that books on the subject would arrive at his door periodically, ordered in secret from online book sites. He'd kept them hidden under his bed, ever since he'd foolishly left one out on the table for Elizabeth to see on one of their illicit coffee dates. She'd been calling him Moon Unit ever since.

So Stuart kept on his quest alone, spending his evenings poring over charts and diagrams, reading all about seven's historical and biblical significance. He lurked in chat rooms on the subjects, though he'd never written anything himself. Even he could see most of the posters were a little nuts.

But it wasn't enough. He wanted answers tailored to his own specific case. He needed a professional, and he'd managed to find one in the city who promised "answers to your most intimate and philosophical questions." Which is why he was currently sitting on a bus heading into the north end of the city and passing streets he'd only heard about on traffic reports. York Mills, Sheppard, Finch, Steeles.

Stuart hadn't been out of the main core of the city, except en route to the airport, in about ten years. He lived for the most part in a fifteen-block radius that took him from the lake to just north of the Bloor subway line, from the CNE to Yonge Street. He occasionally ventured to his brother's house in the east end, but that was it.

He was feeling vaguely apprehensive. He hated buses, with their too-small seats and dirty, muddy windows. He hated that they didn't just stop everywhere like the subway, so that you had to play an active role in getting yourself to your destination. He didn't like not knowing where he was going but had been too embarrassed to ask the driver to tell him when they were nearing his stop. His ancestors used to fight wild animals and other people's ancestors with their bare hands to feed their families or defend their honour. He could barely handle taking public transit to the psychic's house. It wasn't something he wished to give too much thought to.

Adding to his concern was the group of youths standing directly over him on the crowded bus, talking too loud and laughing too hard with their pants half down their asses. Stuart hated teenagers, even when he'd been one himself. They were just so unpredictable. He always harboured the fear that they were talking about him, sizing him up, only to deem him inadequate. An old man, trying way to hard to be young; or worse, not trying hard enough.

Why he cared, he couldn't tell you, but their perceived judgment devastated him. He could be sitting on the streetcar minding his business, listening to the Guess Who and damn glad of it, when he'd see one, in the requisite baggy shirt and bandana, sidle up the back steps looking at him with a knowing "I know what you got on there, Grandpa" sneer. And Stuart would find himself turning down the volume on his personal music device, knowing the next song on his favourite playlist was going to be something by Foreigner.

Or worse, he'd end up sitting beside some skinny fucker looking like he'd been thrown up by Swinging Sixties London in cigarette pants, with a bad shag cut and wearing the expression of someone too bored to live any longer than his sixteen years…and wearing the same tartan scarf and navy pea coat that Stuart himself had on.

And the girls; oh Jesus, these girls. With the nonexistent skirts and the pouty mouths. The ones who were either twelve or twenty-five. Stuart couldn't even think about them. They were fucking terrifying.

In his attempts to take his mind off the fact that one such lovely was currently standing directly beside his seat, her sky-high shoes ensuring his head was directly at crotch level, Stuart was focusing his attention instead on the group of young school kids who were filling a number of the seats in front of him. The thought came to him that it wouldn't do well to tell anyone that he had turned his attention from teenage girls to schoolboys, and once he'd creeped himself out sufficiently to determine there was no malice in his intent, he focused on the two sitting directly in front of him.

They were deep in conversation about an imminent trip to the science centre and all the amazing things they were going to see and do in the hours that followed, when one of them, a little boy who couldn't have been much older than eight, or twelve (Stuart could never really get a handle on kids and ages), sat straight up. He took a look around the bus where he and his buddies were sitting amidst winos and weirdos and said, almost shouted really, "Hey! I'm already ON the adventure!"

It may have been the single best thing that Stuart had ever heard. While he didn't know much, he did know that the wisdom of a ten- or seven-year-old wasn't to be ignored. Stuart sat back, also taking a look around, thinking, *Dude, I'm already on the adventure, too.*

Still, he was very relieved ten minutes later when his foot hit the bottom step and the bus doors opened so he could step out. Freedom. He was in a neighbourhood he'd never been in before, one that looked very much the way neighborhoods tended to look on television. A plaza lined with low, nondescript buildings housing convenience stores and nail salons. Rows of neat tree-lined streets filled with low, nondescript brick houses with asphalt driveways and similar, though not identical, garden beds. An older, post-war neighbourhood built for function and durability. He turned up on of the many streets named for trees until he arrived at 77 Maple St. The address was a key reason he'd picked a psychic so far from his neighbourhood. A close second was the fear that he would run into someone he knew entering or exiting a psychic's place and die on the spot.

The house looked like all the others, which left him a bit disappointed. He'd been hoping for a little more pizzazz from a psychic's house, or at least an old-school shingle out front, covered in moons and stars and written in a gothic hand. He double-checked the address against the printed appointment sheet he'd brought with him and, finding a match, he walked up the driveway and rang the bell. He'd also been hoping for at least a brass doorknocker of some kind, but as he was still trying very hard to believe that he was on an "adventure", he pushed it out of his mind, smiling brightly as a woman opened the door and said, "Welcome, Stuart."

"How did you know it was me?" he said, willing himself to be impressed at her skill.

"You're the only person I've booked today," she answered crushingly, and Stuart felt his cheeks burn a bit.

"Oh, right. I see." As she had already turned around, Stuart's first real impression of her was from behind. She was a middle-aged woman with chin-length mom hair, wearing a tracksuit. This was really starting to suck.

She led Stuart through a tastefully decorated living room into the kitchen, where she directed him to a wooden chair by the table and asked him if he'd like a cup of tea before they got started.

"Ummm..." Stuart hesitated. "Okay. So are we going to do the reading, or whatever, here?" he said looking around the sunny yellow room.

"Yes." She turned and gave him what he felt was a sharp look, asking, "Were you expecting something a little grander? A big ol' crystal ball perhaps?" Then she smiled, which only made Stuart feel more foolish, because that was exactly what he expected.

"Er... No. No. Of course not. I just..."

She came and sat beside him, saying tiredly, though more kindly, "I don't go in for that stuff, though it is what most people expect. It doesn't really do anything you know, it's just a gimmick. I provide a service, not a floor show."

"Oh sure. Like *Medium*..." said Stuart, because apparently the moment was not yet awkward enough for his liking.

"No. Not very much like *Medium*, actually. But I do get that a lot. It's one of the reasons I don't use all that other crap. Hard enough to be taken seriously as it is." The psychic sniffed.

"Right," said Stuart. "Sorry."

"Shall we get started then?" she asked as the kettle began to boil. She stood up to unplug it, tossing two teabags in two cups and bringing them to the table. She didn't ask if Stuart took milk, and Stuart didn't tell her that he did. He was already eyeing the kitchen doorway and wondering if he should just make a dash. Deciding it was best not to anger the sixth-sensed, even an un-showy one, he said simply said, "Okay. What do we do?"

"Tarot reading $45. Palm reading $35. Tea reading

$25, but I'd have to brew you another cup with loose tea for that to happen," she said, making it obvious in her tone that to do so would be a hassle. "Or you can have the works for $75."

Opting to avoid physical contact with a testy psychic, Stuart asked for the Tarot reading. In five flips, Stuart was told that he would live a long life, had already experienced loss but did not yet understand its power, would never be particularly successful in business and might never marry, but would know true love.

Stuart did not know what he'd expected coming to this woman, but he knew he hadn't expected this; to have his life laid out for him by a deck of cards in a matter of minutes by a soccer mom sitting at a kitchen table in the suburbs. Whatever he had wanted to hear, it wasn't what those cards had to say.

The room was quiet as the psychic started collecting the cards, placing them carefully in a neat pile. Stuart wanted to say something to break the silence but didn't know what. He was a bit puzzled, somewhat let down, more than a little concerned that the cards were correct and very irritated that he had just dropped $45 for a few minutes of mediocre news.

Finally the psychic remembered Stuart was there and looked at him, saying, "You do not look pleased. A long life is much more than most can hope for."

"No. That's great. It's just, this, all of this was not what I expected, I guess," Stuart responded by way of apology.

"Sometimes the cards are not kind to us. But they are always honest," she said, standing up to indicate the session was over and it was time for Stuart to go. He wondered if it was the deck that was unkind or the dealer as he stood up, dropping his money on the table, including a sizeable tip, which he resented leaving but felt was necessary, just to be on the safe side.

He hadn't got what he had come for, and while he was hesitant to engage the woman any further, he felt he needed to say something.

"Ummmm...thanks for that. I also came here because I had a weird sort of thing happen."

She looked up at him as she slid the cards back into their velvet bag. "Mmhmm?"

"Well, it's just the day that I broke up with my fiancée, I was wearing a watch. This watch," he said, pulling up his sleeve to show her. "And it stopped that day. At seven o'clock. Exactly." He was looking into her face, seeing her total disinterest turn to amusement when he said, "And so I've been doing a little research, online, about the number seven, and it seems to mean a lot." He was now stammering a little as he watched her eyes light up with the laughter she was trying to hold in.

"Mmhmm?" she said again.

"And so I was wondering what that might mean. The watch I mean. To me." He finished by showing it to her again, because he didn't know what else to do.

"My best guess is that it means your watch battery died," she said dryly, picking up their cups and turning towards the sink.

Stuart saw himself out of the house, down the nondescript street and out to the bus stop so he could begin the long trip home. He made only one stop on the way, to pick up a new battery and a couple of beers. It was the best way he could think of to wind up this particular adventure.

*   *   *

Her name was Randi. She looked like a Randi, all awkward arms and pudge and a nervous grin. Kate disliked her instantly, from the moment she'd seen the girl inching up to her table, knocking against people's chairs and blushing furiously, looking for the least hostile place to land. As Randi noticed the table where Kate was sitting alone, Kate watched her take a deep breath and plunge forward as if she were caught in a strong wind.

"Mind if I sit at this table?" she asked shyly.

"It's a free country," Kate said.

No, actually she didn't. It was what she had wanted to say. She didn't say anything, just nodded in the direction of the chair across the table, a sign Randi took as an invitation to plop down on the chair beside her and flash a megawatt grin.

"Thanks, I just hate coming to these things alone."

"Really. I don't mind in the least," said Kate. Out loud this time. It had just popped out, and she tried to cover the nastiness in it with a smile, then realized she needn't bother. Randi, it seemed, hadn't noticed.

"Well then, you must really be a Woman in Charge!" Randi said in an admiring tone, sending Kate's hand straight past her water goblet to the stem of her wine glass.

"Oh. Yeah. Not really. Yeah, no. I'm here for my boss," Kate mumbled, trying to drain her glass as fast as she could. Kate hated these bi-monthly Women In Charge! luncheons just as much as she hated the Women of Distinction brunches and Legal Ladies networking happy hours.

She didn't come for personal growth, she came because it was her job to do so. Kate was her boss's official seat filler.

Jennifer Davies did not have time to attend hen parties and hated them even more than Kate. She bought the memberships early and often in an attempt to nip any actual communication with event organizers in the bud.

Dear Organization trying to suck up my free time and will to live by asking me to present at your insipid event:
  I deeply regret that I am unable to speak at your luncheon on women cracking the legal glass ceiling or offer a handmade craft for your silent auction due to my hectic courtroom schedule. But as a card-carrying member of said insipid collective, I do support the wonderful work you do in promoting advancement of women in the professional realm.
Yours in sisterhood,
  Jennifer Davies

This left her free of harassing phone calls and inundated with event tickets, which she foisted off on Kate, calling it one of her "other duties as assigned". Kate would always arrive on time with a gift for the hostess from Jennifer, who was always "so very disappointed" that she couldn't be there herself.

To be honest, Kate hadn't been all that unwilling a guest in the beginning. She had found it a rather pleasant way to kill an afternoon, since it got her out of the office and into some of the city's swankier restaurants. She had quite the affinity for these upscale venues, the menus they served, and the free drinks they offered. She liked sitting in fancy places with shiny cutlery and dimmed lighting and mirrors tipped to provide false but flattering reflections. And, due to her lower salary, higher rent costs and lack of wealthy suitors, she had few other opportunities to get into them.

She didn't even mind the speakers they would bring out to inspire her, finding that when she was least expecting it, she *was* a little bit inspired.

What she didn't like about these events, however, she loathed. And what, who, she loathed were the hosts.

She had a most irrational dislike for those cheesy, smug, pointy-shoed women in their mid-price suits and black cat eyeliner. The ones who came up with these horrid luncheon events with names like Women In Charge!

She hated most of the guests as well. Underlings like herself, mostly. Well, not like herself. Like Randi, those frumpy and uncomfortable and hopeful and painfully eager to please. Or worse, far worse, the gym junkies, "super concerned" about the increase in voter apathy, who love fruity martinis and Oprah's pick paperbacks, offering instruction on how to enrich your soul. Working girls who get in early and stay late, proudly sporting the designer pumps they dug out of the clearance bin at one discount store or another and doing their crying on the inside (of the women's washroom, whenever Kate REALLY needed to go).

As if it was so in-charge and clever for a bunch of professional women to get together, dressed to inspire envy and covetousness in their colleagues (and lust in any token supportive male present, the more metrosexual the better). So noble to take the afternoon off from work to come together and eat a third of the chicken Kiev on their plates and stare longingly at the desserts they wouldn't eat (Not me! I'm in Bridal Bootcamp!) and swirl their wine to show off the rings that years of heavy hinting and blowjobs had won them. All the while nodding sagely at each other and affirming they'd come a long way, Sista!

Kate wasn't like them. At all. Sure, she was wearing a lip gloss she'd splurged on at a swank department store make-up counter, but that was only because they don't sell it at the drug store, and it really was a good product. You can't get shine like that from a twelve-dollar gloss.

It wasn't because she was like them. She was a beer drinker. A secret rock star. She watched the news for news, not because the anchor was "sexy in a dad way."

Yes, she was carrying a designer bag she had tracked down in a sample sale. She wore it to show them that she was just as good as them. She could look just as hot and arch her threaded eyebrow just as high. This did, of course, require that she have her eyebrows threaded on a monthly basis. But she *was* different. She actually ate her cake.

Sitting there that particular day, trying at least to look like she was listening to what Randi had to say about what she did for a living, Kate felt that sinking feeling that always came over her when she sat at one of these tables waiting for the food to come so she had something to do besides get lost in her own thoughts.

Why did she come to these things? Was it really because it was work? Then why did she wear her highest heels?

In her heart of hearts, she knew why. With every free white wine spritzer, mini avocado roll and business card prize draw, it was becoming clearer. She was becoming a Woman In Charge! She wasn't original or independent or rock 'n roll; she was a cheap knock-off of the women she despised, and that was probably the only reason she despised them. A non-engaged, non-athletic, non-Brazilianed failure. She wasn't even a good Woman In Charge! She was a Randi.

The realization was crushing. While it was the same one she came to every time she attended one of these events, it did not lessen the impact.

The only difference between this event and the others like it was that instead of a pre-poured complementary glass of wine at each place setting, this event had opted for bottles of wine for the table. Both a red and a white. This was thought to be the right amount of wine for the ten settings placed at each table.

Unfortunately, it was far too much wine for a table consisting of Kate, Randi and the three haughty young women who had joined their table and deemed it inappropriate to drink at a working lunch. By the time the attendees were politely clapping for the speaker, who had started an abused women's shelter, or sniffed out some land mines, or created an ad campaign telling women ugly was okay, Kate and Randi were drinking their own specially-concocted rosé and giggling uncontrollably. It wasn't until a thin and sharp-suited women approached the table and asked her if she was Jennifer Davies' representative that Kate decided whatever it was they'd been laughing at wasn't that funny. She mumbled "No," attempting to cover her nametag with her now wine-splattered napkin. She then stood unsteadily, cursing her shoe choice for the second time and started an unsuccessful attempt to make a dignified walk to the exit. She bounced between chair backs, begging pardon all the way as she tried to ignore Randi's too-loud whispers of "Call me, call me, Katie," carrying over the low buzz of networking women.

She stumbled to the coat check, trying desperately to look sober as she searched her handbag for her claim ticket and fought the panic that was slowly rising through the wine fog.

She was shit-faced. At work. She had made a scene. Had she made a scene? Would they call her boss? Was she going to get fired? AGAIN? Finally she dumped her bag on the counter, sending pens and tampons rolling in various directions, found the claim, got her coat and made for the doors.

Once she had herself safely in a cab, she realized she couldn't go back to work in her current state. She gave the driver directions to her home then grabbed her cell and called Megan.

"Megan Fields."

"Meg," said Kate. "Meg, I gotta go home."

"Katie?"

"I gotta go home." Kate had started to cry.

"Katie, where are you?"

"Meg, I'm sorry. Tell Jennifer I'm going home."

"I can hardly hear you. Are you okay? Are you crying?"

"I'm fine. I'm fine. Tell Jennifer I gotta go home."

There was a pause. "Katie. Are you drunk?"

"No. I just gotta go home," Kate repeated.

"Kate. I swear to god, if you are…" Megan started.

"Okay. Okay. Gotta go. Bye. Tell Jennifer. Okay, bye," Kate said before hanging up.

It rang again almost immediately and Kate almost answered it, trying to figure out how to turn it off. By the time she had accomplished this, she was in front of her building. She shoved some money at the driver, which she later realized could not possibly have been enough to cover the ride, and stumbled up to her bed.

This was where Megan found her hours later.

"What the fuck, Katie?" she said even before Katie had the door open.

"I know."

"No, you don't know. I got you this job, Kate. I told you not to fuck it up," Megan said, stalking into the room and dropping herself angrily onto the couch.

"I know."

"Do you not know that getting so drunk at lunch that you can't come back to work in the afternoon is what most people would call fucking it up?"

"Yes," said Kate. Then, "Does Jennifer know?"

"Yeah, I called her up and told her," said Megan, rolling her eyes. "Of course not. I just left her a note saying the lunch didn't sit very well with you."

"They didn't call her?"

"Who didn't call her?"

"The Women In Charge! people?"

"Not that I heard. Why would they call her?" asked Megan, looking her over with a critical eye. "Did you do something?"

"I drank a lot of wine."

"Yeah. I gathered. But did you do something? Oh

god, you didn't throw up in there or something did you?"

"No. But I was laughing when the speaker was talking."

"Well. That's rude, I guess."

"I think people knew I was drunk."

"Did you tell someone off or something?"

"No. But I just think they knew."

"Tell me exactly what happened."

So Katie retold the details from glass one to glass five.

"Well, I don't think you did anything or said anything too stupid, except maybe to that Randi girl," Megan said, relieved. "I wouldn't worry about Jennifer hearing about it, she doesn't talk to those people unless she has to."

Kate groaned, realizing why that was. "But I do. Oh god, I handle all the calls they make to the office." She sank to the floor beside the couch.

"Well then, if they want to get to Jennifer, they have to be polite to you, regardless of what they might have heard. Don't worry about it. I'm sure it's not as bad as you're making it out to be. But Kate, seriously, what were you thinking getting loaded in the middle of the afternoon?"

"Oh, I don't know. It was those fuckin' career Barbies, you know? They were all just sitting there acting like they were so much better than the rest of the world," said Kate. "They just look so smug because they are so pulled together and so on track to becoming successful, and they just look so pleased with themselves, just sitting there judging me. Like I can't be as good as them. Like I would even want to be like them. I hate those lunches…" she trailed off.

Megan sighed. "Katie, you do realize you do this

every time you go to one of these things?" she said
tiredly. "If you want to be like those girls, go ahead and
be like them, no shame in it. If you don't want to be
like those girls, then fuck 'em. What do you care what
they think of you?"

"Easy for you to say, Meg. You're a professional,"
Kate said sulkily. "You're what they all want to be."

"Yeah, well, so are you, Miss CPA. You are the one
that chose to leave accounting to take Jennifer's calls
and make her monthly waxing appointments."

Katie was silent for a moment, stung. "No, I didn't. I
was fired!"

"Yeah. Fired because you never tried and didn't give
a shit. Listen, you have already worn the suits and got
the bonuses and bought all the fancy dress clothes, and
it bored the hell out of you."

"I just don't like the way they're all thinking they are
so much better than me. Guess I proved them right
today, though. Oh, Meg, I am so embarrassed. I bet
they were all looking at me."

"Uh-huh. Sure. Just like all the cool girls at the
hipster bars are always looking at you and judging you
and examining your every move and ruining your
night, even though you hate all of them too," said
Megan, who by this point had picked up a magazine
and was distractedly flipping through the pages.

"What do you mean?" said Kate cautiously. She had
a feeling there was a point about to be made that she
probably didn't want to hear.

"You spend an awful lot of your time fixated on
what people you portend to dislike think of you, Katie.
And to be honest, it's a huge waste of time."

"Portend? Nice lawyer lingo. No one likes people to think badly of them, Meg. Not even you. You can say you don't care what people think about you when they see you, but everyone cares. Tell me that you wouldn't be as upset as I am if everyone had seen you teetering through that restaurant this afternoon." Kate dropped her head into her hands at the memory.

"Fair enough, I'd be embarrassed. But would I be as upset as you are? No, Katie, I wouldn't." Kate looked up, disbelieving. "Seriously, and that is not because I am better than you or smarter than you, so you can just drop that whole line of thinking for once. It is simply because I understand a key part of human nature that you don't. People don't care about me and my behaviour. People care about themselves. You just let it eat you up, this fear you've got of what people see when they see you. You spend all your time with your stomach pulled in and your face painted on, all the while pretending you don't give a damn about anything, but really terrified that people won't like what they see. And it's such a waste, because no one is seeing you. They may be looking at you from time to time, but they're seeing themselves. So it doesn't really matter if someone notices that you had too much wine at lunch today, or if they had a laugh about it as you were leaving. Or whether you wear your jeans tight enough, or your bangs are chunky enough or whether you opt for stilettos or sneaks. No one is going to bother with you long enough to make that lasting damning impression you are so scared of. No one, in the end, gives a shit, so you might as well just be whoever it is you want to be and not worry about it."

Kate stared up at Megan, a little bit stunned, holding

up one finger so as to have a minute to get her thoughts together. "So what you are saying to me is that I shouldn't worry about what people think about me, because in fact nobody gives a shit about me," she said.

"Exactly," Megan dropped the magazine and slid down on the floor to wrap an arm around Kate's shoulder. "That is what I've been trying to tell you all along."

"Well, Megan. That is just a world of comfort."

April

In Japan, purple is the colour of poison. In Toronto, it was the colour of Stuart's very tiny bathroom. This was not his choice. He hadn't gotten around to repainting the bathroom, or any of the large unadorned walls in his new loft. Not yet. Aside from the few nail holes he and Graham had filled and the coat of varnish they had put down on the floor to ward off splinters, Stuart hadn't done much at all. But he was going to. He had plans.

"I'm planning to put some pictures up. I've been working on some new pieces for the space. I know how it looks," he said as he ushered Elizabeth through the spacious and sparsely-decorated living room and into the kitchen.

"Of course," she replied, just as she'd replied during every visit she'd made since he'd moved into the place in early December.

"I mean, I know what you're thinking," he said. "Six months, and it still looks like a warehouse or something."

"No, no," she soothed. "I think it's nice. It's…roomy."

Stuart was not convinced. "I know you think I'm not committing to this whole 'change your environment change your life plan', blah, blah, blah. I know everybody is thinking that. But I totally am. Not that the whole commitment thing has worked out for me so far, ha ha." He poured her a cup of coffee from the impressive-looking espresso machine on the counter. The elaborate chrome and eagle-topped contraption had been a ridiculous purchase that he and Emily had made when they'd first moved into the condo. It had been their first joint purchase. It was the only thing he'd taken from his last kitchen.

As far as Elizabeth could tell, it was the only thing he had added to the new one.

It was like that all over the house. Bare rooms spotted with odd and impractical remembrances of his life with Emily. A gilded music stand holding wet towels in the bathroom, something they'd found in an antique shop outside of the city. A large oak humidor Stuart was using as a TV stand in the bedroom, one he'd found on the street that Graham had helped him to refinish. A wrought iron garden bench tossed with mismatched linen pillows in the living room, where he was now directing Elizabeth to take a seat since there wasn't a proper chair in the place. This they had bought on sale one day, even though they didn't have a yard to put it in. They'd bought it for the yard they were going to have when they bought their first house.

"So, speaking of horrible failures," Stuart said as Elizabeth wriggled to get comfortable, "have you talked to her lately?" He said this far too brightly to convince her that he wasn't desperate for news.

In one of those strange "you're shitting me" twists of fate, it turned out that Elizabeth was the long-time lawyer of the man Emily was now married to. Elizabeth had found this out in a most uncomfortable pre-nuptial session, when Emily had waltzed through the door of Davies and Associates with her lawyer in tow. It was a standard-issue agreement. No quarrels, very cut and dry. Perfunctory was the word that came to mind. *Très romantique.*

Elizabeth had been so thrown that she'd called Stuart up and told him all about it, something she had regretted deeply ever since. He had not taken the news well. No one likes to find out that they were the practice spouse.

"Stuart, honey, I thought we agreed to skip this whole nightmare topic," she said wearily. She'd tried to say it humorously, forcefully and even pleadingly in past visits over the last few weeks, but with very little success. Stuart had become fixated. He had been with Emily for years before they had even moved in together. Now, in six months, she had met, moved in with and completed all of the legal paperwork needed to marry another man. He had tried as hard as he could, but he could not get past it.

"Yeah. Sure, whatever. That's totally fine. I don't even really care; I was just asking to be polite… And, you know, because she was only the freakin' love of my life and one true soulmate," he added with a lopsided grin that would have broken her heart if she hadn't begun to steel herself against it months ago. So she simply changed the subject.

"How's work?"

"Work's work."

"How's the painting going?

"It's going."

Oh for two. Elizabeth could feel the tension rising in

him. If she didn't get through to him soon, he'd either get up and punch something or put his head in his lap and cry, which would be much worse.

"Okay, how's your volunteering coming along then?" she asked.

"Oh, that's delightful." Elizabeth held her breath, but Stuart continued. "I show up, slap on my natty headset, tell a few people that maybe they shouldn't off themselves, pat myself on the back and come home." He stretched his long legs out to meet the upturned wine rack-cum-coffee table.

"Well, that just sounds like hell." Elizabeth was still far from sure that his decision to work at a teen hotline was a healthy one, though it was the one thing that continued to get him out of the house.

"Don't you think it might be a bit more cheery to work with happy kids or dogs or something?" she asked him yet again, trying to make it sound casual to hide her concern. In her current pregnant state, she wasn't very good at hiding things like that.

"Oh, don't worry," Stuart countered, reading right through the question. "If I was going to kill myself, I'd do it because I've been left to wallow alone in my own thoughts and misery. Not because some fat fucker in Etobicoke can't get laid and hates his gay father," he said testily. There really was something emasculating about the fact that all the women in his life thought Stuart was a key candidate for suicide. As if he somehow wasn't tough enough to stand his crappy life. He'd been standing it for the last six months, hadn't he?

Seeing what he thought might be tears in the back of Elizabeth's eyes, he quickly altered his tone, saying,

"Besides, if I ever got that low, I've had two weeks solid training in how to talk myself out of it."

As close as he was to her, and she was the person he'd been closest to his entire life, closer even than Emily, they weren't the kind of friends who cried in front of each other. Yelled and moaned and complained, yes, but not cried. They weren't huggers either. As soon as they had decided they'd be better off as friends, they hadn't really been physical. It was the only way to keep up a friendship with an ex, and even now that she was pregnant and married, Stuart wouldn't feel comfortable having to wrap his arms around her if she burst into tears. Didn't want any chance to look back down that road and wonder at all what he might have given up because he hadn't fought harder to keep her. They were better as friends. He knew that. But he had always been a little bit in love with her too. It was better that he keep his distance and avoid holding her, or having any contact that might upset the balance and send him off chasing his married best friend and closing the door on the best relationship he had ever managed to maintain.

But he'd do it, of course, if she needed it.

Fortunately, she didn't. She blinked once, then twice, then said dryly, "Well, that is comforting, Stuart. That's really comforting."

They sat there in silence for a minute, Elizabeth savouring the earthy smell of her coffee, eyes closed and nose buried in the cup, Stuart watching her out of the corner of his eye, hoping she'd soon say something to stop the uncomfortable thoughts that were running around in his head.

She took a long, slow sip, sucking at the rim of the cup like it was a cigarette. Then, sighing contentedly, she opened her eyes and turned her attention back to him. "So that's your current activities taken care of. What's the next topic of conversation you'd like to bring to a screeching halt?" She wriggled her body forward to dislodge a metal rose from between her forth and fifth vertebrae.

Funny. They were back to funny. Stuart was so pleased, he decided he'd actually make an effort. "Ummm, how about health? Let's see. I went to the doctor for my physical on Tuesday. So far, no doomsday calls, and for the first time in six months, I had someone caress my balls without my paying for the privilege. Thank you OHIP!"

"Oh, Christ. Well, that covers your sex life too." Elizabeth shifted a little farther to her side of the bench, even though she knew his not-so-secret fear of hookers meant that he was lying. She didn't make a joke about it, though, which both of them would have expected. It left a silence in the room that made them a little uncomfortable, a bit sad.

"Yessiree. We are just whipping through this visit, buddy," he said in an attempt to fill it.

"Well, it does help that you haven't bothered to make any inquiries into my health or wellbeing."

"Oh. Sorry. I have been wondering… Pregnant or just bloated?" he said, looking over at her mid-section.

"Hilarious."

"Seriously, how are things in utero?"

"So far, so good. We have another ultrasound scheduled for next week."

"Can you get photos of that?"

"Uh-huh."

Stuart turned in his seat so he was facing her directly.

"Can I ask you a personal question?" he said, almost solemnly.

"Wow, two in a row? I'm flabbergasted, let her rip."

"You're sure this is Michael's, yes?" Elizabeth stiffened, and her eyes narrowed, so he quickly continued. "There's no chance it's mine?"

She laughed, surprised to find herself surprised by anything that came out of Stuart's mouth.

"Well, seeing as we've never had sex, I'm thinking it's not," she laughed, relieved. He was kidding her. This is what they did, Elizabeth and Stuart, they kidded each other. This was normal.

"I guess. Though you do use my toilet. A lot. Every time you're here. And maybe sometimes in my excitement, I've missed the mark a little?"

She laughed again. More than laughed. She snorted. "Okay, so now I am picturing something I should never have to picture, and I am a little nauseous. What I am not, however, is carrying your baby, which you would know if you had paid any attention to the public health nurse in sixth grade."

"Pity," he said seriously, looking around the room. "If it was mine, you could send me the ultrasound, and I'd have something to hang on my wall. Maybe I'll be the godfather?"

"No chance, jack-off Johnny. What kind of role model would you be?"

"That's fine talk from the pregnant woman gulping

down a double espresso. I wouldn't want to be any kind of father to your junkie baby anyway."

Stuart knew he'd pushed too far as she said, "Okay, so maybe it's better when we do only talk about you." Because even though she smiled as she said it, she set her coffee down on the humidor with enough force to rattle his empty cup.

"Okay, sorry, not funny."

"It's fine. I'm sorry, I know you're kidding. It's just, well, we're not really talking here, are we? We're not ourselves. I'm not used to being strange around you, so careful."

"You don't have to be careful. I'm fine." He was worried for a second that he had been right all along in his assumption that she could read his mind. But looking at her, he realized she was talking about her concern over his bare walls and dirty dishes in the sink, his feelings for Emily.

"I don't know that you are fine," she said.

"Well, I'm trying to be fine."

"I don't know that you are trying."

"Well. Jesus, I'm… I miss her, Liz."

"I know you do, honey."

"Yeah? Well, she doesn't miss me. She's moving on. And you, you're moving on. Fuck, look at you. Last fall I was in a four-year relationship, planning a wedding, and you were single. Now you're pregnant, married and seeing to my ex-fiancée's pre-nup so she can have a hassle-free divorce when things go south. Six months, and everyone's world has changed, and I haven't hung up a single picture."

"And?"

"And? And it's not fucking fair."

"Not fair."

"Yeah, not fair. I mean I'm sitting here without a fucking clue, and everybody else's life is just lining right up for them. I'm stuck here, and I don't even know which picture to hang on which wall, even though I am or I pretend to be a goddamned artist, and everyone else is just happily living their lives according to plan. Do you know what I would give for a little of that? To fall asleep for once and know that what I am doing is what I am meant to do? To know I have at least some of it right?"

"Stuart," Elizabeth said quietly, "people don't live like that."

"Some people do."

"No." Elizabeth shook her head. "No, they don't. Life is not better to some people than others. It does not treat some of us more gently or with more favour. It's a total myth." She put up a hand to stop him from interrupting. "Some people just tell you they have a handle on it so that they can call themselves the winners. They do it so you will feel like shit. They do it because they are fucking liars."

"Says the woman living in the house with the husband and the summer home and the baby on the way," he said, waving his hand in her general direction and rolling his eyes, wishing away what she'd said, because he didn't think he wanted to think about it right now. It had been a cheap shot, but Stuart didn't seem to know it, so he was totally unprepared for what Elizabeth was about to say. It's like that with men and women sometimes.

"You want those things? Go get them. I'll tell you how. First fall in love with a guy at fifteen, stay with him until you are twenty-one, until the day he tells you he is leaving you for one of the many, many women he has been having sex with since you met. It's not your sister, and not your friend, though he nailed them too, it's the one he knocked up. The one in your undergrad program.

"Then decide you can't take it any more and drop out of a school that has given you a scholarship, leave your family and friends, all to get away from the expanding belly of the woman who stole your life."

The colour was rising, and so was her voice. Stuart could see her knuckles turning white as she held firm to the lip of the bench. He opened his mouth to say something to calm her down, but before he could make a sound, she shot him an angry look, saying, almost hissing, "No, Stuart. No. I'm not done. You want to know how to live my life? I'm going to tell you. Where was I? Right. After that, you move to a new city and go work at a coffee shop for minimum wage for six years so you can afford a dumpy little apartment in a shitty end of town and scrape together enough money, along with a crushing student loan, to pay for tuition and food and replace your electronic equipment each of the THREE times it is stolen, once by the next guy you decided to let into your life.

"During that time, you'll have to bury your grandfather and personal champion after he falls off a ladder cleaning the goddamn gutters and snaps his neck.

"Then you go to work one day, start talking to a guy and realize he's the first man you've had a laugh with in two years. Give him your phone number. Go on a first date. Go on dates two through ten. Get drunk, forget to use a condom and get pregnant. Find out that instead of being horrified, you both think it's sort of terrifyingly cool. Discover that you are still having a laugh. Move into the house he bought with his cousin. Head to City Hall to get married so your mother doesn't die from shame, and Bob's your uncle. In my case, literally." She released her grip on her seat to place it on her mug so she could drain the last precious drops and catch her breath.

Stuart was gaping. It had been a while since he'd seen her this fired up. It was the first time she'd ever talked to him about why she came to town. When they had met at the party of a mutual friend, she had just said she was in need of a change.

"I don't know what to say. I didn't know. I'm so sorry. You so deserve your happiness."

Elizabeth sighed. She heaved the breath and all its meaning upon him. "No, I don't deserve anything. You are missing my original point here. I had some shitty times. We all have shitty times. We all have good times too. That is my point. Life is not some merit contest. Life is just fucking life. Regardless of what happens to you along the way, you can have a happy one or a sad one, depending entirely on whether you are more comfortable being happy or sad. And you can't control everything that happens to you. You can't ensure your future any more than anyone else can. And those smug bastards that run around feeling like they have one chosen path and are following it blindly to bliss really piss me off. To sit there and say 'I was meant to be a social worker and can't imagine doing anything else.'

Well, shut it. You could be just as content, given the right circumstances. If you can't imagine it, you just have no imagination, it's not that it isn't possible." She leaned back against the metal, looking a little exhausted.

She'd given him a good talking to, and while it hadn't been pleasant, it had been enough to show him that, in her way, Elizabeth loved him too. He wanted to give her something for her effort, to be able to tell her that all of that talking had convinced him of something, but if he were honest, it hadn't, and he wanted to be honest with her.

"I don't know if I can believe that, Liz."

"Well, you don't need to believe it for it to be true, Stu," she answered as she stood up and headed for the bathroom.

*   *   *

Their paths had crossed occasionally at the courthouse, but it was during the negotiation of a pre-nuptial agreement that they had first gotten a chance to talk. The couple was ridiculous, both young professionals with barely any assets, trying to ensure on paper that their true love was never in a position to steal their crappy record collections.

Afterward, they'd ended up at a nearby bar, declaring that if they didn't need a drink, they deserved it. He'd asked for a beer, and when he told the waiter to save a glass, the bottle was fine, her heart had fluttered, which surprised her immensely.

They'd chatted and sipped, exchanging cards at the

end. And she'd waited, anxious and miserable for him to call, which he finally did two weeks later. They'd gone to dinner, then to his place, and she'd never really left.

One night after they had both decided that an extra bottle of wine was not excessive, but necessary, Michael had taken a long drink and asked a question that he'd felt too stupid to ask her before. "Did you like me right away?"

Too comfortable to be coy about it, Elizabeth said, "Yeah. Pretty instantly."

"Then it seems pretty antiquated that you just sat around and waited for me to ask you. Not so thoroughly modern, are we, missus?" He was jocular now that his suspicions were confirmed.

"Oh, fuck off."

"No, really," he continued, all glib confidence. "This surprises me. You can stand up there in front of a room full of people and win yourself a court case, but you couldn't ask a man, an obviously interested man, out for a drink? What gives?"

Elizabeth thought about laughing it off, but something in the way he looked at her, the slightest crinkle in the corner of his eyes, made her think that she could let him in on the deep, not so dark secret. She could let him have this.

"Okay, I'll tell you," she started, draining her glass and hoping that any slurring on her part wouldn't take away from what she was about to say. "There have been a few events in my life, times when I have gone disastrously out on a limb chasing one boy or another. They weren't many, I guess, an awkward phone call here, a drunken email there, a few obvious misreadings of friendly gestures. You know. He didn't shut the door in my face, he loves me too! So no boiled rabbits or anything, but still, they were attempts at love, at which I failed miserably."

Michael nodded slowly, not totally sure what turn the conversation had just taken.

"So these moments, small as they may seem to everybody else, the cost of doing business or whatever, are burned into my long-term memory. I trip over them occasionally when I'm trying to dredge up the ingredients in a Bloody Mary or the name of the other Marx Brother. And if I stumble upon one, it plays itself out in technicolor in my head, and I can't stop it, and I'm right back there in that moment putting myself out there for nothing, and then I just die all over again."

Elizabeth looked and saw him staring at her with an odd expression. She sat up, intending to steel herself from whatever stupid, funny comment he was about to make and cursing herself for allowing her past embarrassments to set her up for a brand new one. But Michael said nothing, and when she forced herself to look at him again, she saw confusion, not amusement. He was trying to think of something to say, but not having much success, so she continued.

"So here you are. This guy I like. I mean actually really, really like. A guy who's smart and funny and who drinks his beer right out of the bottle, even when he's in a designer suit. And you are all packaged up in this pleasing form, with dimples to boot, and I was smitten enough to know that I never wanted to have to think back on meeting you and want to die."

She finished with an offhand shrug, trying to make

the whole thing seem like simple fact and not deep disclosure. She willed him not to make a joke. She wasn't sure what she wanted him to say, but she knew it couldn't be a joke, even though she'd given him all the material in the world, and she wasn't sure in a similar situation that she would be able to resist. What he said now, even in a bit of a wine haze, was going to determine what became of Michael and Elizabeth, and she knew it.

He sealed their fate by saying nothing. By answering, "Well, 'nuff said," then taking her to bed. That was the night Elizabeth got pregnant, which they confirmed together a few weeks later after the ten sticks Elizabeth had peed on all turned blue.

They were surprised by the pregnancy, of course, but even more so by the fact that they were both pretty happy about it.

They'd gone to City Hall and been married a few days later. Her mother had been appalled. They told no one but Stuart who, along with a bailiff, had been the depressed and unwashed witness for the union.

The next few months had gone on in a happy, bloated blur, until the day Elizabeth came across an old photo of Michael's parents' wedding and started to cry. Sob, in fact. Big, gulping sobs. Michael came in to see what the problem was, expecting to find she'd dropped a plate or caught sight of a puppy or something. She was all-over hormones and had begun to cry at just about anything.

She held up the picture saying, "This baby will have no pictures of us dressed up like assholes to share with their friends." She was distraught, like maybe this issue was not entirely based on estrogen, that her heart might actually be breaking.

Pregnancy was a strange and scary time for a man, at least a man like Michael. It had been a period of wonder and fear and guilt in which his job seemed to be to get in the way of things and apologize a lot for the fact that he could still be thin and eat sushi, and regret that he'd had to put her through this so that he could end up with an heir.

A lot of the time, Michael felt entirely useless. But this, unlike the sweater she'd thrown away in a fit of cleaning and now missed desperately, was something he could do something about. He dropped immediately to one knee and said, "Marry me, baby...you know, again."

∗　　∗　　∗

Whatever that photo had meant to Elizabeth, what it meant to Stuart was that he now needed a date. While this renewal of the vows was initially envisioned as a rather overdressed barbeque in the backyard, Elizabeth's mother would have none of it. Having been denied what she felt was a motherly right the first time, she was insistent that this wedding would be done "properly". Since she was equally insistent on paying for it, Michael and Elizabeth happily acquiesced, Elizabeth even agreeing to go with her mother to buy a gown from "Great Expectations", the wedding dress store for the promiscuous bride-to-be. Though that was not actually part of the sign on the store. Elizabeth had found the experience to be much more to her liking than past trips she'd taken to wedding shops in bridesmaid capacity. "None of this 'wait six months for your dress' crap. They know the shotgun's loaded and ready to go. You walk out with your polyester number the same day!" she'd told Michael when he asked why he was no longer allowed access to the bedroom closet.

Knowing his options for a date to be limited, Stuart had considered everything, from randomly asking the next girl he saw in the elevator to trying to contract some sort of communicable disease that would make his attendance impossible. He had even thought about signing himself up with an online dating site until he'd mentioned it to his mother on the phone one day and heard such a scathing opinion of the "people who resort to those sites", that he had been scared off.

He knew he did have one choice, a fun and pretty one at that. He could ask Kate. She knew Elizabeth, was fun to hang out with and wasn't seeing anyone. She was also the only single girl Stuart actually knew. So aside from bringing his mom, if Stuart wasn't going to show up solo, he was going to have to ask Kate to the wedding.

It wasn't really a big deal. Friends ask friends to weddings all the time. He was fairly confident that at this point he thought of Kate as a friend, and that she thought the same.

"So really, no problem," Graham said as Stuart tried to convince them both that asking her would be totally no big deal. They were sitting in Graham's tiny backyard enjoying a beer and one of the first half-decent days of the spring. They had to wear coats, but they were still outside, and after months of being trapped indoors, Stuart was happy to feel the warm, watery sun on his face.

"No. It's perfect."

"So why haven't you asked her to be your date then?"

"Ummm. I'm going to, but it's not a date. Well yeah, she'll be my date, but it won't be a date. Not a date-date. I'll just ask her to go with me."

"Yeah. I wouldn't ask her like that. Unless she is already under the impression that you are a twelve-year-old girl," his brother said, ruining a great putdown by continuing on to the heart of the matter and asking, "Dude, you aren't into her, right?"

That was the question. Well, not really a question. The way Graham put it, it was more of a statement. And it was true. Kate and Stuart had already determined they weren't attracted to each other. Not really.

But the longer he was on his own, and the more comfortable he became around her, the more he thought that maybe they should be. She was the best thing to happen to him since his break-up, and the older he got, the less likely it was that pretty, fun blonde girls were going to skate right up to him and tell him they thought he was awesome.

Before he could explain any of this to his brother, Graham continued. "Because you know, it never ends well when you make a play for your friends."

"What are you talking about?" he asked, though somewhere deep inside, Stuart was aware that he knew exactly what his brother was talking about.

"Oh, let's see, Emily, that Lisa chick from high school, oh um, Elizabeth."

"I was never in lo—"

"Oh, come on, you have a thing for Elizabeth, and

you know it, everybody knows it."

"Graham, that's not true. We only dated for like six weeks, about a million years ago."

"True. But that's only because she didn't want to date you any more, not that I blame her. But if she was still into it, you'd probably be married right now."

Stuart didn't reply. What could he say to that, except that it was probably true? He just sat there letting it sink in and wondering how crappy it was going to make him feel to have to look that little fact in the face days before he watched her marry someone else.

Then Graham spoke again. "That doesn't mean you'd be happier, Stuart. You guys really are better as friends." This Stuart knew was also true.

"And what do you mean it didn't work with Emily? We were together for years. We were almost married."

"Yeah, *almos*t is the key word, buddy. Listen, I'm not saying you don't give it your best effort when you get into these relationships, I'm just saying in the end they don't work out. Well, okay, except for Liz. You guys are cool. But you haven't even heard from Emily again since she dropped off that stuff at your place, have you? And she did it when you weren't even there. Like, she fell out with you and didn't even tell you about it for months. You were pretty decent about it, considering, but she hasn't even talked to you since. I wouldn't say that whole relationship was a big success."

Graham said all these things with the calm assuredness of one of those carnival knife throwers. Stuart took the news like one of those carnival knife throwers' lovely assistants, with a smile plastered onto his face, stuffing all of the fear down as far as he could.

"What are you trying to tell me here, Graham?" Stuart grabbed the neck of the bottle he was drinking from and wondered how it was that he had never been the advisor in this relationship. Graham kept his own counsel, and the decisions he had made, good or bad, had been entirely his own. It was always Stuart sitting at the knee of his little brother, trying to figure life out.

"I'm just saying that if you want to bring this girl to this wedding so you don't go alone, that's fine. But dude, if you bring her home after the wedding so you are not alone, you are going to regret it. If you guys try to force yourself into a couple, it's just going to blow up, and Stu, no offence here, but you don't really have a lot of friends to lose these days."

This all made a lot of sense to Stuart, even if he didn't like it. He knew the temptation that a couple-heavy setting and open bar presented. Especially when he'd be sitting beside the closest thing he had to a girlfriend.

But the thought of showing up at the wedding as the third wheel to Graham and Jane, then sitting with a bunch of single lawyers to fill out an odd-numbered table was awful. He was torn.

"So I shouldn't ask her?" he said, nestling further into his chair and waiting for his brother to weigh in, expecting the worst.

"Ask her if you want, Stu. Just don't fuck her is all I'm saying."

In the end he didn't have to. Ask her that is. Kate called him later that day, saying that her friend Megan had asked her to go to the wedding as her date. She didn't have a man to ask and didn't think she could suffer the single lawyer's table either. While Kate was up for going, she had called to tell Stuart it would be his duty to flirt at least a little with each of them, since it was hard enough for an older single girl to gain the attention of a man without everyone thinking she was a lesbian. For all of the wise things that Graham had said to him earlier, it was the skewed logic of two single women that saved a friendship.

* * *

For a woman about to be married in the morning and in labour shortly thereafter, Elizabeth was in fine form. She was relaxed and smiling, even in the face of her mother's month-long onslaught of opinions about floral arrangements and entrance music. As she got ready for bed that night, Michael was watching her. He was nervous, and she wasn't, and he wanted to know why.

"We're getting married tomorrow," he said, trying to elicit some sort of sympathetic nervous response.

"Can't wait. Night baby…and baby," she said, kissing his cheek, patting her stomach and rolling on to her side.

"So you're going to sleep?"

"Yeah, honey, I'm not really up for it tonight, you know?"

"No, I don't mean that. It's just…we're getting married tomorrow, and the baby's practically a guest."

"Uh-huh."

"So how can you just roll over and go to sleep?"

"Because I'm tired. I am content and well fed and in love and very, very tired."

"Well, I'm tired too."

Elizabeth rolled over as quickly as a very pregnant

woman can to have a look at him. "But you aren't happy? You're not about to jump ship here and leave me on my wedding night eight and a half months pregnant, are you? Because that would be really bad form."

"Of course I'm happy."

"You do realize that we are already married, yes?"

"Yes."

"And that this is basically just a big party, and that once tomorrow is over, nothing in our lives will have changed?"

"Yes."

"And you are telling me that you are happy about this?"

"Of course."

"Well then, good night."

"I just don't get how you can be so blasé about this happiness. Honestly, a year ago I didn't even know you, and now we are not only a family, but an expanding family. Seriously, a year ago I didn't know your name and now… Why aren't you staying up in fear about it going tits up? Honestly, it'd make me feel better."

Elizabeth heaved herself into a sitting position and took hold of Michael's hand. It was warm. He was always warm. She loved that about him. Since they'd been dating, she'd even stopped wearing socks to bed. She looked at him for a moment, trying to wake herself up and get her thoughts together.

"I'm not worried, because I have chosen to believe, improbable as it is, that love is not rocket science, and there is no great mystery to it. Babe, sometimes life is just good to you. Sometimes things just work out. It's that easy."

These were the kinds of things that she could now say to Michael. Things that sounded so hopeful and new-agey that never in her life had she said them to anybody else.

Michael thought they were new-agey too, but he loved to hear them anyway. Tonight, however, he wasn't entirely convinced. "But how do you know that this is one of those times? How do you know that this is the big love? That the search is over, if you'll allow me to quote Survivor."

Elizabeth laughed. "First, I thought we agreed no arena rock in the bedroom. And as to how I know that this is the love to end all loves?" She stopped for a moment and took a little breath. It was ridiculous how soft being with him had made her. Not *made* her really, these thoughts had always been there. Elizabeth had always wanted to root for the good. It was ridiculous how being with him had made her feel it was okay to be soft. And now she was going to tell him something cutesier than anything she'd spouted so far. Cutesy and true, and she thought he needed to hear it. "Well, I know it because this is how I thought love would be when I was nine."

"Oh. Right, of course. All cleared up."

"I wasn't done. You know how when you are little, you think growing up will be so great, because once you're really old, like twenty, you'll be a grown-up and know how to do things like mix a drink and talk at parties and feel confident about everything, including love?"

"I vaguely recall the feeling, yes."

"It makes you think the things you have to go through, like getting boobs and acne and losing your summer holidays are a fair trade?"

"Generally. But I'm hoping not to get my boobs until I'm at least forty-five."

"Shut up. Well, now I'm in my thirties, and I rarely feel confident about anything, and I can't make a drink that doesn't come out of the bottle pre-mixed."

"I'm afraid you are contradicting yourself here."

"Would you hush? See, I met you, and it was love, and I'm sure of it. No maybes, no cold feet, no ifs, no buts…okay, a largish butt, baby weight I swear. And it's just like I thought it would be when I was nine. So, it turns out *you* are what it was worth getting boobs for."

She could feel all his tension flooding out through the fingertips she was gently massaging. While she was thankful the lights had been out while she made her rather embarrassing speech, she was glad that she had told him. It seemed to work.

"That is, without a doubt, the single best thing anyone has ever said to me in my whole life."

She smiled. "So, do you think you'll get some sleep now?"

"I just might."

"Good, because I desperately need my beauty rest."

"Ain't that the truth?"

Her smile grew. As endearing as was with his worrying about the future, this was the Michael she wanted with her weeks before she was about to be a mother. She brought her hands up to his face and kissed him once slowly on each cheek.

"You are such an ass," she said.

* * *

Since no one really cares about the details of weddings they did not attend, a quick recap will suffice. The day was sunny, the bride beautiful, the groom calm. Michael used Elizabeth's boob line in his wedding vows, thrilling and embarrassing her to equal degrees. Seeing them together made Stuart a little sad, but not because he wished they weren't together. It was simply the fact that seeing them together, in the moments they thought no one was looking, or didn't care if they were, Stuart had to admit to the possibility that true love might in fact exist. Not for everyone, mind you. That was the sad part.

For all of that, he'd had a pretty good time escorting in his opinion two of the hottest girls at the wedding. One of the lawyers, whom no one would have guessed had any sense of humour, had seen them together and started calling Stuart "Pimp Daddy". As the night went on and the drinks flowed, the name caught on, as did the unfortunate tendency for their work colleagues to refer to both Kate and Megan as "Pimp Daddy's Hos". The insult was assuaged by the fact that all of these men would spend the next week living in fear of the lawsuits sure to be filed against them.

In the later hours of the evening, the three of them had left the party and headed to a nearby pub for a final drink, or three. Here the conversation turned towards relationships. By the end of the night, they had decided that Graham was right, and Stuart and Kate should remain friends. As for Megan and Stuart, who had really only hung out for the first time that evening, there was still a window of opportunity for a hook-up. They were still discussing the pros and cons a few pints later, Kate dutifully listing each point in the appropriate column on a napkin, when they decided they couldn't decide if they'd make it or not and would have to leave it up to fate. Heads, they would never speak again; tails, they'd get married immediately, leave the city, open a raw milk dairy farm and spend their remaining years creating delicious cheeses for the black market.

May

In the seconds immediately after he received the phone call, Stuart confirmed there was a God. In truth, he less confirmed his belief in Him than chose to believe. He needed someone to blame, and the baby wasn't big enough. A baby didn't have enough weight in this world to hold the amount of rage that Stuart wanted to unload. He needed someone, something, bigger than the world itself.

So he chose to accept the Lord God into his heart and let loose a howl. One loud and wounded enough to wake up the man who lived in the apartment below, sending him running up the stairs to find out who had died.

It was Elizabeth.

Stuart finally opened the door to stop the incessant knocking. When he said aloud that Elizabeth was dead, to the man who had never even once held the elevator for him, Stuart felt something shatter. He felt the splinters shooting in all directions. Felt them in his fingers and his bowels and behind his eyes.

He could see his neighbour gesturing at him, could see his mouth moving but heard nothing but a high buzzing in his ears, like the sound cicada bugs make in the trees when it gets too hot. But he was not hot. He felt a chill, could feel it creeping up his arms and legs. And he felt heavy, his muscles trembling under his weight.

Then he didn't feel anything for a while.

Having never fainted before, Stuart was embarrassed to be told that he had done so, pitching backward into his apartment, knocking his head on the doorframe on the way.

His embarrassment turned to humiliation when he realized the ammonia smell causing his nose to wrinkle was not smelling salts but urine. Stuart had pissed himself in the hallway of his apartment and in front of his neighbour.

With some effort, he managed to sit up so he could look at this stranger, one Armstrong, Kenneth, if his mail slot label was accurate. Stuart wanted to apologize for his inability to in any way control his earthly vessel. But looking at the man, he saw something that made him forget the wet and the stink and the shame. It was the way his eyes had gone soft in the corners, his eyebrows lifting, and the slight nodding of his head. He was the one who looked sorry.

Then Stuart remembered that Elizabeth was dead.

He didn't know what to do about it. He didn't have a fucking clue. He sat staring dumbly into space as the minutes passed. Kenneth, Ken to his buddies, finally asked if Stuart thought he might be able to stand up. So Stuart stood up.

Then he asked if Stuart might be more comfortable in fresh clothes. So Stuart turned and went back into the apartment, into the bedroom and over to his dresser, pulling out a pair of jeans and a T-shirt.

Ken, suggested gently that maybe he'd want a quick shower first, but Stuart looked back at him with eyes so forlorn, causing him to say quickly "Never mind about it", and to ask instead if he might poke around the kitchen for something to tidy up the hallway with. Stuart nodded.

Ken fled to the kitchen, thankful for a task he could do away from the shell-shocked young man in the next room and the ghost of whoever Elizabeth was.

He didn't know much about this kid, who'd moved in recently and made no attempt to be friendly with any of the people in the building. Ken didn't know if Stuart had a wife or girlfriend, or boyfriend for that matter. A quick look around made him guess that Stuart lived alone, but he really couldn't say for sure. One thing he did know, the boy was in a bad way.

Ken had seen the look Stuart had given him before, sadly more than once. He'd been in the service and spent long periods in one crap hole or another, keeping the peace. He'd seen that look in the young men away from home. Boys who didn't know that you could be so frightened by noises in the dark and didn't know you could walk around with a hole in your chest, asking for help and a cigarette.

He'd seen it since then as well, too often in recent years. Coming from the watery eyes of men as old as he was, with wives who had quietly kept their lives worth living. Men who were supposed to die first but didn't. Men who were utterly lost. He'd seen it in his own eyes for the entire year after his Anna had died. Still saw it there sometimes.

He hated that look. It was worse than anything you'd ever see on a woman's face. A woman's grief had grit in it. Women had a talent for suffering. A woman's grief was full of purpose. Whether tender or furious or self-abusive, their sorrow had strength.

Men, when they let go, when they let it in, were flabby and frail. Weak as children. Helpless. Finding a mop in the crevice between the refrigerator and the wall, Ken dampened it in the sink and carried it over to the door, leaving a trail of droplets behind him. Covering the wet stain Stuart had left on the carpet, he scrubbed with fury, exorcising all evidence of the urine, the incident, the look.

He wished he were a heavier sleepier, that he'd never gotten up. That he hadn't had to be a part of this event. It wasn't his. He wished it as much for Stuart as for himself, and he knew that once he had finished, he would return the mop, say his goodbye, shut the door and never speak of this again. It was the best way.

Ken debated announcing his departure from the hallway, but in the end he popped his head into the bedroom to make sure the boy was still standing, so to speak.

He found Stuart sitting on the bed with his head in his hands, his sodden pyjamas on the floor near his feet. He was breathing heavily in short, hard bursts. He wasn't crying, yet.

Before he had a chance to start, Ken told him that he'd "cleaned up the mess."

Stuart didn't say thank you. He didn't say anything. He didn't move. Ken wasn't even sure he'd heard him. That was fine. A heartfelt thank-you would have been just one more embarrassment.

"You might want to have that head looked at…son,"

he said. Stuart was rubbing the back of his head, roughly. Ken thought it must hurt. Whatever was going on with this kid, it must hurt like hell.

He'd added the "son" to try and sound sympathetic, but it had come out foreign, even to his own ears, and he wished he could take it back.

Stuart lifted his head, still breathing hard, still saying nothing. Staring almost blindly but directly in Ken's direction.

Dammit, Ken thought, feeling trapped, unable to leave. *What am I supposed to say? What else can I do?* He didn't know this man, didn't know this Elizabeth woman. He wanted out of this room, away from this wound. He wanted his heart to stop wrenching. He wanted a drink. He was desperate.

When the phone rang, he almost jumped out of his skin. Stuart did not answer it, but his gaze drifted in the direction of the sound, breaking the spell.

Ken turned quickly, heading for the door, stopping only to look over his shoulder and say "Sorry for your troubles" in the formal tone used for wakes and sympathy cards. A sense of order restored, he hurried out of the apartment, down the stairs and home. Safe.

*   *   *

Stuart wouldn't pick up his phone. Glynnis had tried three times before tossing on her coat and grabbing for her lipstick. As she looked at herself in the mirror, she stopped. A woman dead, her son unresponsive, and she felt the occasion required lipstick? She was not herself. She'd only just received the call and was hardly awake.

She hesitated, the tube in the air, unsure. Should she or shouldn't she put it on? She was not herself. The tube did not seem real in her hand, like some other object instead. It was the shock.

The young die, of course. Everyone knows the boy who drove off the road, or fell through the ice or got some strange inoperable tumor in high school. Everyone has their "I knew a girl with cancer" story.

But the young die fiercely. Bombings in the Middle East and right here at home sometimes. They perish of horrible diseases in third-world humanitarian camps, swallowed by tsunamis or liquor or depression or lust.

In that you could find, if not solace, then satisfaction. They were spectacular ways to die.

But this? To bleed out slowly while having a baby, in a sterile hospital room in the city, surrounded by doctors and nurses and your Doula and your spouse? To die and leave the tiniest little baby behind you? Never to know that he was born and that he was your son. Never to know what his name would be in the end.

In the end it was Gus, after her grandfather, although previously Michael had sworn he'd never allow it. He'd done it for her. Not that she'd know it.

This was unspeakable, inconceivable, the depth of this sorrow.

Just so fucking unfair.

You weren't supposed to know people like this. This you were supposed to hear about in some grey-toned and weepy Irish play or in an old woman's remembrances. Glynnis had thought these kinds of things didn't happen any more. Not here. Not to people she knew. She'd had herself convinced.

178

She put the tube down, shaking herself, and headed out of her apartment towards her boy who needed her. She got there to find the door unlocked and the hall carpet wet. The place was so still, she thought for a moment he might not be there at all, but she found him in the bedroom, his head in his hands. She stood a minute looking at him and wishing desperately that her aunt or her sister, or even Graham were here. It wasn't Tylenol he needed this time, or a shoulder to cry on. She didn't know what it was he needed. She was afraid of him.

Realizing that no one else was going to come, that it was really up to her, she walked silently to the bed and sat down beside him, her purse in her lap as if she were at the doctor's office. She hoped he'd say something, hello, anything. Just acknowledge that she was there, but he said nothing. She turned on the lamp on the nightstand and noticed the trickle of blood running down the back of his neck.

"Oh, honey, what's happened?"

He said nothing at first. The silence stretched out for seconds, all the while Glyniss holding her breath, then she heard him mumble, "Elizabeth."

"Oh, yes, yes I know. Her mother called me after she spoke to you. She was worried when you hung up. Poor thing, she has enough to worry about already." Then, watching Stuart stiffen, she added, "I'm sorry. I didn't mean... I didn't mean anything at all."

He said nothing.

"I am so sorry," she tried again. "It's awful. So sad. The poor little one. The family."

He still said nothing, leaving her to flounder

through a string of platitudes. He wasn't going to help her with this one. She was going to have to be a good mother all on her own this time.

"You're bleeding, it looks…" she faltered, reaching out to touch his head.

"It's fine." Her hand froze in mid-reach, stopped by the warning tone.

"How did it…?"

"I fell."

It was a roadblock as much as an answer. He did not want her here. She could not be anywhere else. She had no idea how to comfort him, what this loss meant to him or why he should be this upset. The friendship had always been a mystery to her; an oddity full of sarcasm and clever comebacks. She'd never heard them really talk, never understood that that was how they did it.

She looked at him, pleading for him to look up and see that she was trying. He didn't. They sat in silence. She wished again for Agathe and Helen. People who would make him see them, someone who even this kind of grief would not ignore.

She stared longingly at the phone and knew a few quick calls would summon all the troops. But turning back to her son, she knew that noise and fuss and pre-made meals were not what he needed. Not now.

What Stuart needed now was someone to sit with him while he stared into this dark ugly night and tried to hold on until morning. Someone who would just shut the hell up and hold his hand and try not to drown in the waves of silence and the onslaught of tears. Stuart needed more than she had ever given anyone. And what Glyniss needed was a backbone.

"Stuart. Stuart, you have to look at me, honey."

He didn't move.

"Stuart you need to look at me. Please."

No change. She wanted to cry. She wanted to run home and pretend she'd never gotten the call. Instead she grabbed his chin and forced his head up. "Stuart. Look at me. I'm sorry, honey. I am so sorry. I don't know what else to say. I don't think there is anything else to say. And I don't know what to do for you. But I want to take a look at your head." He tried to shrug away from her, and she struggled to keep hold of him, feeling the nail sink into the soft skin under his unshaven chin as she leaned around and gently parted his hair to see a surface scratch and an angry welt forming. "I'm going to put some ice on this, Stuart, and you are going to let me because…because you have to."

He winced and nodded almost imperceptibly, but it was there. He had heard her. She had proven to both of them that she was there. Then she went into the kitchen to get him some ice.

June

It was seven in the morning. Exactly. He'd watch the cards fall over on his old roll number clock. 0 7 0 0. He had been watching them fall in minute intervals the entire night; at first from the bed then from the chair by the window. There was nothing to see on the street, which was fine. He wanted to watch the clock.

He hadn't been sleeping, and when he couldn't sleep, he watched the clock.

It wasn't new. It was entirely new.

He used to watch as a form of meditation. It was something to do when you weren't doing anything. Now he was watching with purpose. He would not be late.

7:01. He stood up, feeling the pain in the muscles that ran along his spine, and took his first steps towards the bathroom. Standing in the shower, he counted the seconds it took for the water to run from freezing to too hot. It took almost one hundred and eighty seconds. He didn't adjust the faucet. He was focused on the cleaning. All the bits of himself usually left to the mercy of stray droplets were meticulously scrubbed. Between his fingers, behind his knees, under his toenails. He scoured his ears and shoulders and the cleft of his ass. His skin turned pink, then an angry red.

He didn't stop until he saw that he'd drawn blood on one shin.

Grabbing a towel to wrap himself in, he stepped to the sink, wiping the vanity mirror with his forearm. He'd turned the fan on, forgetting that it didn't work. The room was still full of steam that clogged his head and dampened his towel, leaving him no drier for having put it on.

He filled his palm with shaving cream, making a cloud of it, an alpine peak. It was too much. He slathered what was needed on his face, leaving his lips uncovered, a gash in the snow, sending the rest down the drain with a wet slap. As he grabbed his razor, the expensive silver one, the one he never used, he noticed he was shaking. He set it down, staring at himself through the vapor. He took a minute to steady himself, then looked out the bathroom door to the roll number clock. 7:26.

*   *   *

7:26. She was awake. The alarm had gone off at seven, but that was not what had woken her. She could sleep through anything. It was Tracy who'd woken her, at the foot of the bed yelling that she shouldn't set the fucking alarm and wake the goddamn house if she was just going to ignore it. Kate had asked her to stay over the night before because she was nervous about today. Due to a combination of good genes, good luck and relatives who lived at great distances, Kate had never been to a funeral before.

Turning it off, she knew she had to get up, but she didn't. She waited, watching the second hand circle and

circle the large vanilla face of her wall clock. She counted
to eighty then stopped. She knew this was going to put her
behind schedule. She knew she would be cursing herself
for the rest of the morning, but still she didn't get up.
Paralyzed. Sinking deeper into the luxury of wasting time.
There was an opulence about it, a ridiculous grandness,
like setting fire to money or feeding the dog champagne.
She needed to get up. It was a very important day.

But that is not why she got up. In the end, she rose
because she knew that if she didn't pull herself from
her womb of flannel and brushed cotton at that very
moment, she might never get up. And she had
promised Stuart she'd be there.

This logic was the same that got her up most
mornings. Because the other option, to lie catatonic for
hours waiting for the day to come to a merciful end, was
generally the more appealing one. Kate was aware this
didn't reflect a positive life outlook, and it seemed almost
sinful to be wasting away her life on the day of Elizabeth's
funeral. Not the actual burial. That had been taken care of
in a flurry in the days after the baby was born. No time to
do anything public then, new life trumps no life in the
world, it seems. So today her husband and family had
invited those that had known Elizabeth to a memorial of
sorts, having finally found the energy to say goodbye.

As always, Kate had been tapped to go in Jennifer
Davies' stead, her boss having been called away
unexpectedly to some made-up function. Jennifer
hated funerals even more than charity luncheons.

Crossing the cold pine boards on the way to the
bathroom, Kate reminded herself that she was really very
lucky. Lucky to still be here, to have the choice to get up

and walk across this room, to feel the coolness of the central air and blink at the pure sunlight streaming through the window. Tracy had already put the coffee on, and the rich aroma was so strong, Kate could smell it wafting from the kitchen. She was lucky, she told herself, then as if to confirm it, she said it out loud: "Lucky".

Then she sighed. She hated when she did this, this roll call of blessings. She didn't feel lucky; she felt defeated. This sense of despair in the face of so many good things made her feel sulky and childish. She hated that too. She had never been one for looking at the bright side when she didn't damn well feel like it.

She fumbled for the bathroom light and swore when the fan came on instead. The noise was too much, too grating. Switching the switches, she was greeted with silence and light.

The thought entered her head that "Silence and Light" would be a great title for a song or a book—if she ever wrote a song or a book. She immediately pushed it out of her mind. It was too early for that kind of noise as well. She began the process of getting ready.

She stared in the mirror, taking stock of what she had to work with. She looked good, she thought. Tired and pretty. She wondered if it was shallow to be thinking that kind of thing in light of what the day held, but she was so rarely satisfied with what she saw that she decided to let herself have the moment. She reached for her toothbrush.

She knew she wanted to wear a suit. A dark one, but not black. Black seemed too much. To intrusive for someone who wasn't close to the family, too familiar for a work associate. Besides, she wanted something fitted.

She needed to feel encased. Her skin didn't seem capable of holding her these days, and she wanted reinforcement. Ever since she'd heard about Elizabeth and the baby, she'd felt bothered. Small and a little lost. She didn't like being made so obviously aware of how out of control she was, how out of control everyone was.

Kate slid on a grey skirt and matching jacket, feeling like she was going to a sales meeting. She didn't think it was right, and she did want to look right. She wanted to make up for the fact that she had seriously contemplated not going today, even though she'd been ordered by Jennifer to go. Even though she'd borrowed Tracy's car and offered Megan a ride. Even though she'd promised Stuart she'd be there when he had to tell stories about his dead best friend.

Kate had some making up to do, even if no one knew it, and she was going to start by not fucking up her outfit.

She was taking off the skirt as Tracy came in the room, somewhat subdued with a coffee in hand. "Sorry about the yelling," Tracy said, passing the cup over. "I forgot you had the thing today." They had been calling it the "thing" since Kate had found out about it.

"I don't know what to wear," Kate said, staring into the depths of her closet, hoping to spy the right thing.

"Don't ask me. I've never been to one of these things either." Tracy stared into the closet for a minute herself before saying, "You'd best wait for Megan, she'll know."

And of course she did. Megan arrived twenty minutes later, wearing a subtly patterned sundress and black cotton sweater. Kate couldn't help but think for the millionth time that there are some people in the world who have their shit together. Following Megan's example, Kate quickly grabbed a simple shift out of her own closet. "Are you scared, Meg?" she said, sliding it over her head.

"Scared?"

"Uh, sad, I mean," Kate responded, blushing a bit as her head popped out the neck hole.

"Yeah, a little. Elizabeth was a nice girl, and then you know, the baby and everything. It's a sad thing," Meg said. "Are you sad…scared I mean, Katie?" she asked with a little grin.

"Oh, shut up. But yeah, a bit. I mean, what am I supposed to say to these people? Her husband? I didn't really know her. And what if the baby is there? Am I supposed to say nice things?" Kate asked, the questions coming out in a rush. "Or what if I start crying or something and embarrass myself? Oh god, what if I laugh or something? I've heard that people sometimes do that."

"Say what you feel, and if you cry, you cry," said Megan, grabbing Kate's purse and ushering her towards the door. "You won't embarrass yourself, barring wine bingeing at the reception afterwards," she added, giving Kate a little hug. "Oh, calm down, I'm joking. You'll be fine as long as we get out of this door and into the car so we aren't late. It's a bit of a drive, and we're behind schedule." She checked her watch.

9:02.

*   *   *

9:02. Stuart was standing on the porch in front of his brother's apartment, trying not to ring the bell again. He looked at his watch that now kept perfect time.

9:03. He reached for the bell again, just as the door opened and Graham stepped out to meet him.

"Sorry, couldn't find my goddamn tie," Graham said, holding it up as evidence. "Then I couldn't remember how to tie it, and Jane nearly choked me to death trying to do it for me. Can you do it?"

Stuart grabbed the tie, tossing it around Graham's neck. As he worked the knot, it occurred to him that this was probably as physically close as the two of them had been in a long time. Graham cleared his throat, then asked, "So, how are you doing?"

"Fine. It'll be fine. I don't have to talk if I don't want to." This was the line he'd been repeating to everyone since Michael had asked him if he'd like to say something at the service. He'd immediately said yes but then began to panic about what he'd say. After his fourth semi-frantic message back to Michael leaving possible poems or song quotes on the answering machine, Michael had assured Stuart that he could speak or not speak, that it was cool either way. They would play it by ear. And while he'd since had something ready to go, he'd still been holding on to that sentence like a lifeline.

"Dude, you'll be fine," Graham said, waiting patiently for Stuart to finish with the tie. Once he did, they stood there for a few seconds longer, but with the task completed, it felt awkward. They weren't the kind of brothers that hugged. Stuart let his hands drop and cleared his throat, and Graham fished the keys out of his pocket, saying, "Let's hit the road."

* * *

10:45. That was the time on the dashboard clock when Kate pulled into the parking lot. She had been worried the entire ride that they would be late, but as they sat in front of the nondescript United Church, she was afraid it was actually too early. There weren't many other cars in the parking lot. At least none she recognized as belonging to people from the office. She didn't want to be the first of the guests to arrive; the eager mourner who makes polite idle chit-chat with the people who really knew and loved this woman. Finally Kate said, "Well, we can't just sit in the parking lot. It looks ridiculous." So they got out of the car, making their way to the heavy wooden doors. The church was not the kind of church Megan and Kate were used to. It was a simple brick box with little adornment, no steeple and not a bleeding Jesus or beatific Mary to be seen shining from any multi-coloured window, no bones of long dead saints out on display.

This made Kate even more nervous. While not particularly religious, she liked her faith served up with a heavy side of tradition, gilt and limestone, dark wood and solemn silences. It added a sense of seriousness to things, which she found comforting. Walking into this place, which looked a little like her neighbourhood copy shop, would make the ceremony about to take place feel even more surreal.

"If there is a sing-a-long or a 'hug-it-out' session in here, I am going to freak out," Megan mumbled, perfectly summing up Kate's fears. Before she could respond, she turned to watch a cherry-red old-school convertible turn into the parking lot. She was relieved to see Stuart sitting inside. But as Kate watched the car pull into a spot in the far corner of the lot, she realized that she didn't really know what she would say to Stuart once he got out. She turned quickly back towards the doors and headed inside.

Graham and Stuart had ridden in silence for most of the trip, and that had suited them both. They could spend long periods comfortably in each other's company without saying much. That was the kind of brothers they were. Today this was especially useful, since Stuart had some final tough decisions to make about the memorial. It wasn't that he didn't know what to say; that had never been the problem. He had always known exactly what that right thing to say was, he just didn't know if he had the guts to say it. He had tried to come up with suitable alternatives. Something better, more gentle, more suitable to the occasion. The trouble was that what suited the occasion would not suit Elizabeth. Not at all. He didn't know this instinctively, or because they had been real, true friends. He knew it because Elizabeth had told him so.

It wasn't a message from beyond the grave or anything, or even something said with a touch of foreboding or foresight on Elizabeth's part. It was said years ago one night over beers, when the conversation after a lazy dinner with Graham and Jane had turned to death.

If you are going to talk about death, the perfect time to do so is on a wintry night when you are safely tucked away in your home having just had a nice dinner with friends. When the things most likely to take you out, hunger, the elements, loneliness, have been thoroughly staved off.

The foursome had already talked about how they

would prefer to die, "while sleeping" being the unanimous response. Then they covered the worst way to die: buried alive for Stuart, burned for Jane, Shark attack for Graham. Elizabeth had said drowning, because how could she know? After they had discussed what they wanted to accomplish before it happened, the conversation had turned to what each person would want to happen if they could plan their own funeral. It had been silly talk really. Stuart had said he wanted a kegger. Jane requested her husband put her in the ground wearing all the jewellery her mother had given her, to keep her sister's grimy hands off it. Graham had said something funny and vulgar that Stuart couldn't even remember. But he remembered Elizabeth's explicitly. In fact, as soon as the shock of her death had diminished a little, it had popped into his head, and he hadn't been able to stop thinking about it ever since.

It was not appropriate. It was said under the influence of too many beers, and partly to try and top the ridiculous things the rest of them had come up with. But there was something in the way she said it, how delighted she was with herself for coming up with it. How much it epitomized all that she was, had been, that made Stuart firmly believe that nothing else would do her justice.

As they stepped out of the car, Stuart's mind was made up. He looked over the white canvas hood of Graham's car and asked, "Do you remember the night we all had dinner with Liz at your place and talked about how we wanted to see our final goodbyes?"

Graham squinted at him from across the car, like he was preparing himself for an unpleasant piece of news.

He slowly drawled, "Uh-huh."

"I think that's what I'm going to do for Liz today. I think that's what she would have wanted me to do." Stuart said it firmly, hoping against hope that Graham wouldn't tell him he was an asshole. Not that it mattered now. His mind was made up.

"Christ, Stuart," Graham said almost under his breath, staring at his older brother for a minute, trying to determine whether he was serious or not. But he already knew Stuart was. He leaned his arm in through the window and popped the trunk, saying with a shrug, "Well, that explains the stereo." Stuart sighed and walked around back to grab an ancient tape deck. The brothers walked silently towards the church. They were almost at the doors when Graham suddenly stopped and grabbed Stuart's arm, saying, "I'm sure you're doing the right thing here buddy, or at least I'am sure that you're sure, and you knew her way better than I did. But just for the record, regardless of what I may have said to you in any previous conversation, I do not, and I repeat, do not, want to be waked in an open casket stripped naked and with my nut sack pierced, no matter what kind of rise it would get out of our mother."

"Ah, the piercing. I knew yours had something to do with your scrotum," Stuart said, laughing and grateful that Graham had made the hardest steps he had to take today a little less so. Regardless of how everything went down from here on in, it would all work out in the end.

As they made their way up the aisle, Stuart tried not to catch anybody's eye. He did notice Kate sitting with Megan at the end of a pew. He gave a little smile he wasn't sure she saw but didn't stop until he'd arrived at the front

of the church at the bench behind the family, where
Michael had asked him to sit if he was going to speak. As
he slid into the pew, Michael turned around to greet him.
If he noticed the stereo, he didn't say anything, and his
expression was unreadable as he thanked them both for
coming. He was holding in his arms a wriggling bundle
he introduced as Gus. His son. Elizabeth's son. The reason
they were here today, Stuart thought, hating himself for it
almost instantly. It wasn't true. It was true. But it wasn't
right to say it, even think it. It was the kind of thing his
mother would have thought, and a terrible, terrible onus
to put on someone so little, who hadn't asked for any of
this in the first place. While he tried to process all of these
thoughts, the smile drying on his face, Graham leaned
over to meet the little man, lifting him gently over the seat
and covering with grace Stuart's awkward silence.

"Named him after Liz's grandfather, god help him,"
Michael said, a bit of a smile flitting across a tired face.
"I had been dead set against it, since he's not a ninety-
year-old man. But Ellie wanted it, and well…"

Stuart looked up at him, a bit startled to realize he
hadn't known that the baby's name was Gus. In the few
times he'd spoken with Michael since Elizabeth had
died, he'd asked about the baby, surely, but it had
remained "the baby".

"Quite a boy, isn't he, Stu?" Graham said, staring
pointedly at his brother. Then, turning to Michael,
adding, "He looks like his mother."

It was the right thing to say. Graham had a gift for
knowing the right thing to say, and Stuart watched the
satisfaction Michael took in agreeing with him. But as
Stuart shifted his gaze from Michael's face to the

baby's, to Gus's, he realized it *was* true. Something in the shape of the eyes, or the chin, or maybe even the hands now wrapped tightly around Graham's index fingers, was Elizabeth. Stuart was captivated, and whatever bad thoughts he'd been having about this baby and himself for feeling them faded as he reached out a hand to touch Gus's fuzz-topped head.

"Watch the soft spot!" Michael blurted, in surprising unison with Graham, who had instinctively placed a hovering hand over Gus's tiny head.

Stuart's hand shot back, and he mumbled an apology as Michael reached for his son saying, "Sorry, Stu. I've had so many people warning me about that damn spot that I'm getting a little paranoid."

Stuart nodded. Not sure of what to do next, he turned to Graham, asking, "How do you know about babies' soft spots?"

"Everybody knows that, buddy."

The minister made his way to the altar, signalling the start of the service. Michael turned around again this time, raising an eyebrow in the direction of the ghetto blaster. "You have something to say today, I'm guessing?"

"Yes."

There was a pause as Michael studied him a minute. "Okay. I'll have you go last, if that's all right with you," he said, his face still unreadable. "In case whatever you have planned turns out to be a show stopper." Then another tired smile broke across his face before he turned around.

As the service began, Kate's church anxiety began to wane. She stood when others stood and sat when they sat. She was grateful to find there wasn't a lot of congregant participation to worry about. The service itself was quite nice, as these things go. Not a lot of strangled tears and mournful speeches. Elizabeth's family spoke simply and warmly, their remembrances leaning towards funny stories that let you know exactly what she had meant to them and how much she would be missed. Even her husband's brief talk thanking them all for coming to say goodbye to Elizabeth and hello to Augustus wasn't as sad as it could have been. It seemed that maudlin behaviour would not have been tolerated by Elizabeth, and that was respected.

All in all, Kate would have to say she was almost enjoying herself, which sounds worse than it was. She was sad certainly, but it wasn't that desperate unhinged kind of sorrow that can run you through. This was more of a slight ache, one you've earned after a hard day's work. It was a satisfying kind of sad. When Elizabeth's husband stepped down from the altar, Kate had already shoved the remaining Kleenex from her travel pack back in her purse and was fishing for her sunglasses when the minister went back to the podium saying there was one final speaker who had a tribute to make.

Kate watched Stuart stand up, still in his trench coat, which was really too hot for the day. He made his way up the few steps at the front and turned to face the attendants. She saw the black box at his side and started to get a little nervous as she watched him adjust a few knobs before standing back up.

"Oh, god," she said, turning to look at Megan. Just when everything had been going so well, he was going to go for the cheap tears?

"What is he going to do?" Megan whispered into her ear, pinching her arm a little, like she was somehow responsible.

"I have no idea," Kate replied, slapping her hand way.

"If he plays 'Tears in Heaven' or some shit, I'm going to lose it," Megan said tightly, obviously concerned that Stuart was about to ruin her clean escape from the emotional hostage-taking of most funerals.

Oh, please, please, don't do anything awful, Stu, Kate thought, willing him to hear her as she watched him pull a piece of paper out of his pocket, unfolding it once, then again.

He stared at the paper, collecting his thoughts for a moment, then cleared his throat before calling out:

"Dearly beloved…"

"Oh, god," Kate said again.

"We are gathered here today…"

"Oh, please God," she said, fighting an urge to run from what she was sure was about to turn into a sentimental nightmare.

"To get through this thing called life…"

"Oh…"

"Electric word, life. It means forever, and that's a mighty long time."

"My…"

"But I'm here to tell you. There's something else. The afterworld."

"…god."

"A world of neverending happiness, where you can always see the sun, day or night."

"Katie, is that…?"

"So when you call up that shrink in Beverly Hills,

you know the one: Dr Everything'll Be Alright."

"Katie, it's Prince!"

"Oh, my god"

Katie and Megan looked at each other, shocked if not yet horrified, then looked around to see what everyone else was making of Stuart's performance. Kate noted the odd person cocking their head as something familiar caught their ear, but for the most part people were silent and watchful. Kate looked back at the front of the church to see Stuart standing there, hands and voice trembling a little as he read off the paper. He looked small up there in his oversized raincoat. He looked a little scared. She couldn't believe he would use this time to take the piss, but she couldn't figure out what else he was up to.

"Instead of asking him how much of your time is left, ask him how much of your mind, baby."

Stuart stopped, staring over at Gus inadvertently. Though when he thought about it, he guessed he was speaking to him as much as anybody. This little person who had been on the road to becoming a fixture in his daily life, a part of his inner circle, who would have called him Uncle Stuart, because Elizabeth would have insisted on it. Who would now probably grow up not knowing him at all.

Then his gaze widened to take in Michael and Elizabeth's mother and a few other people who had been a part of his life and would now be out of it. They were looking back at him, some blankly, some with concern, and others with that look on their face that you get when you are trying to puzzle out where you'd heard something before. He didn't know if what he was doing was going well, or if he should stop for the sake of those present. But he wasn't really doing it for them. He was doing it for Elizabeth, who would have loved this. Who *was* loving it, wherever she was. Not many people might know that about her, maybe Michael, or Graham, or maybe her sister. Though from the look on her face, he doubted it. Well, this was a part of her that mattered, had mattered to him, and it was his only chance to let them all know. To tell this collection of acquaintances he would inevitably lose contact with. He mustn't falter.

So, carefully avoiding Michael's eyes, he turned back towards the machine sitting at his side and pressed play as he swung it up over his head, saying to Gus, and Michael and Graham and Elizabeth. To himself: "'Cuz in this life, things are much harder than in the afterworld. In this life, you're on your own."

And it wasn't seamless, but it was close to it, as Stuart stood there, legs spread, stereo held high in all his Lloyd Dobbler glory and let Prince tell the congregation. "If the de-elevator tried to bring you down, go crazy."

Kate watched, mesmerized, as he held the machine high in the air, letting the song play out over the huffing and tsking and angry confused whispers of the mourners. It was ridiculous, what he was doing. Ridiculous that they were all there in a church remembering a woman who died tragically in childbirth, and her final goodbye was a teen movie parody and an Eighties club tune. But Kate couldn't help smiling, because it was kind of awesome. There were going to be a lot of people who hated him for pulling a stunt at a funeral. But there was something about it that touched Kate more than any of the other comic and wistful tributes she'd heard all day. When the song ended, the church was dead silent, all eyes still focused firmly on Stuart, who didn't even blink as he lowered the machine, nodded to the first pew, where Elizabeth's husband was sitting and, as far as Kate could tell, laughing into his son's hair, and walked down the centre pew out of the church.

After the door had closed quietly, the minister snapped to attention, and as he ran to the pulpit to thank everyone for coming and directed them to the church hall for refreshments, Kate turned to Megan, trying to find a way to sum up what had just happened. But all she managed to say was "What the hell was that?"

"I don't know, Katie, and I'm guessing this really isn't the time to be asking about it, but is Stuart still single? Because coin-tossed fates be damned, that guy is pretty rock 'n roll."

July

K ate hadn't realized that she'd been working at Davies
and Associates for a full six months until she
received a voice mail telling her to make sure to be on
time the following Monday, because Jennifer had slotted
an hour for her probationary review. Kate was not
looking forward to it. She hadn't made it past a six-
month review in any of her past three positions. Granted,
she hadn't tried very hard in those jobs. Hadn't had
Megan threatening to kill her if she didn't. She knew she
shouldn't be too worried about getting fired. She'd
managed to fly pretty well below the radar, sucking up
just enough to seem useful but not cloying. She stayed
late when she thought she ought to, even when all she
had to do was order her groceries online. She kept her
desk and her computer cache clean. Aside from getting
drunk that one time, she hadn't done much to call
attention to herself, and even that seemed to have missed
Jennifer's attention.

She liked to think that her boss would have had a
laugh about it anyways, because deep down Kate
thought that Jennifer was sort of cool. Formidable and
a little scary yes, but she'd seen the look her boss could
give sometimes to hapless people saying stupid things

without knowing it and was pretty sure the woman wasn't made entirely of steel.

Of course, Kate was too afraid of her to test the theory, so as she sat on her bed that morning surveying her wardrobe, she was not planning an outfit for work, she was selecting her battle gear. In her past two jobs, it had been during probation reviews that the truth had come out about her lacklustre performance and poor work ethic. That was the day to pack up the plants and personalized pens and to breathe in the sweet air of freedom. But this was going to be different. Hopefully. Kate didn't want to get fired this day. She liked her new office, if not all of her assigned duties. She liked the people and the case discussions and the mini-internal dramas and, god help her, she could now admit it, even dressing up for the inspirational lunches. She wasn't ready to go yet. She wanted to go into that meeting and come out with her job. And the benefits available to all full-time staff, including massage.

Kate had risen extra early that morning to make sure she had enough time to get herself together. No clockwatching. At seven thirty, she was well into her second cup of coffee and trying to convince herself it was not too early to call her sister, which of course it was.

She was surprised to find herself missing Scott then. She'd hardly thought of him in months. But it was at a time like this that being alone was just so inconvenient that she wished desperately she had him here to wake so as to discuss these morning preparations, to calm her down and listen to her worries and help her pick the right sweater—he'd always had an eye for that kind

Kerry Kelly

of thing. She could now consider herself well over him, but feelings like this did come over her from time to time. She found it so strange that the things she missed about him weren't the things she expected to miss. It wasn't his strong arms or great smile or ability to stay calm when driving through inclement weather. It was stuff like his taste in women's work wear that brought him to mind. Just thinking about it made her feel alone, and that made her feel lonely.

She jumped up from the bed, trying to shake the mood. She was already nervous; add lonely to that, and she'd be bawling through the interview. If she knew her boss like she thought she did, Kate would be better off spitting in Jennifer's coffee than crying in front of her.

She went to the closet for a final scan before deciding on black pants, a grey dress shirt and a white sweater. Adding a belt and a ring, some boots and other necessary paraphernalia, she turned to have a look in the mirror. She looked long enough to scan for any missing buttons or obvious stains or holes. Just long enough to decide she looked professional and put together and that the white brightened up her face, which had looked a little tired when she'd stepped out of the shower. But she looked no longer. Any longer and the whole works would start to crumble. Look too long, and that's when you see the little things about yourself that you can't stand the sight of. Suddenly you're not standing so tall or looking so good, and the whole outfit is wrong. Once you are looking with that critical eye, you know there isn't an ensemble in the whole world that would be right. Not the one you loved yesterday, not the one you always looked great in

202

before. You will have nothing to cover up your innumerable imperfections, and you will end up leaving the house in sweatpants.

So Kate turned quickly from the mirror, carefully avoiding it during the rest of her preparations, and left the house thinking she was looking pretty good and deciding it was safe to hope that she wasn't about to get fired today.

More than that, Kate found as she walked out the front door of her apartment onto a sunny sidewalk that she detected, somewhere in the back of her mind, a sense of purpose. Today was a day she would actively get things done.

She not only wanted to keep her job, she wanted to *do* it. To clean out her email inbox and create a functioning calendar to keep track of Jennifer's court dates, instead of writing them down on various sticky notes. She wanted to look into updating the information on the company Intranet that still listed Jennifer's assistant as Lorraine Simmons. She wanted to create a personal out-of-office voice mail message to replace the one generated by the system.

By the time she'd stepped off the streetcar in front of her office, Kate had created a "To Do" list of over a dozen items that she was now clutching like a security blanket with one hand as she fished for her security pass with the other. Riding up the elevator, she tried to quell the fire that had sprung up in her cheeks with a few deep breaths and managed to look only slightly pink by the time she sat down at her desk, dropped her bag and noticed a crisp manila envelope from Jennifer leaning against her monitor. Inside was a note saying she had been called out of the office for the rest of the day and that Kate's official review would be rescheduled.

The note went on to explain that as her contract was up at the end of the week, in the meantime Jennifer had also left her a new one to sign, which was neatly clipped to the back of the note. It wasn't effusive, or even polite, but the note said all that it needed too. Kate had done it. She had kept a job. And she'd managed it with no horrible review, no awkward chatting, just a simple form to fill out and fax to the Human Resources department. A form that noted she was now a full-time staff member, with benefits. She was a valued member of the law firm of Davies and Associates. She sat back and looked at the list she had created, of all of the things it was still within her power to do. She looked them all over, underlined and prioritized as she turned on her computer, popped open the internal messaging system and clicked on Megan's contact name.

"J.D. is out for the day. Up for a coffee break?"

*   *   *

Stuart wasn't feeling sad. At least not typically sad, or at least what he thought of as typically sad. It was true he hadn't left the house much since Graham had dropped him off after the memorial service, but he wasn't sitting around in tears all the time. He hadn't been binge drinking or anything like that. In fact, he'd dumped most of the liquor in the place a few weeks ago. While it had seemed fitting to sit around and get pissed after

Emily had left him, it didn't seem cute this time to be too much alone with his thoughts and a bottle. The last time had scared him a little and made him feel selfish and a child.

Once he'd taken care of that, he actually thought he had gotten on quite well. He was content to be at home. It didn't hurt to think about Elizabeth as he'd thought it might. He even found himself smiling if he caught himself doing something he thought she'd remark on, or heard something on television that he knew she'd roll her eyes about. He thought of her often, not really as she was in the end, a wife or mother, or a corpse. More as his partner in crime who'd gone off on some great adventure. A Peter Pan to his Lost Boy.

When Emily had left, he had felt a huge hole in his life, in himself. He had missed her like crazy and missed all he thought might and should have been. He didn't feel like that with Elizabeth. She wasn't gone. He found her everywhere. He even talked to her sometimes, about his day or something he'd read in the newspaper.

He was still reading the newspaper. He hadn't become a hermit or anything, tuning the world out as he'd done before. He was just taking a little time out. It was comfortable to be at home having the occasional chat with his best friend, feeling close to her when he did so. The talks were one-sided. He didn't hear her responding, hadn't become delusional, though he was fairly sure she was listening. He talked to her in the same way he used to talk to God when Agathe would have him kneel down and pray in her attempts to save his soul from Glyniss's lackadaisical agnosticism.

"Dear God," he had always started. Then he would proceed as in a letter home from summer camp. "How are you? Thank you for the trees and flowers and our food. Please make me taller than Graham again. Thanks, Stuart Lewis."

He had been pretty sure, even at a young age, that this was not the way that other people prayed. But since he'd been too embarrassed to ask anyone how it was really done, it was how he had continued until he gave up on it entirely sometime in his mid-teens.

This was now how he found himself conversing with Elizabeth, although slightly less formally in his salutations and sign-offs.

"Heya, Elizabeth. How are you? I'm okay. Meant to go out to the store today but never got around to it and am now forced to eat tuna out of a can. Who knew I even had a can of tuna? And not just the one, I found four cans on the top shelf of the cupboard. I don't even know if I bought them and don't want to think too hard about how long they have actually been here. But desperate times as they say, oooo, speaking of Desperate, I'd best be getting myself over to the TV before I regenerate any of those brain cells I worked so hard to kill off playing video games earlier. Here's hoping it's not a rerun. Later, Stu."

It occurred to him afterwards that he might actually have been praying to her, though at the time it just felt more like one of the lopsided conversations they used to have when he would ramble on about some topic she had no interest in while she nodded, not listening, and flipped through a magazine or something. They'd had plenty of those.

So Stuart wasn't sad, and with Elizabeth's silent presence, he wasn't lonely either. Not like he had expected to be. In fact, Elizabeth was such good company that Stuart hadn't realized he had hardly spoken to anyone else since the memorial. A few people calling on work-related issues and a few food delivery people; a telemarketer or two. He had been vaguely aware of the constant flashing of his message machine light informing him of an ignored call from his mother or brother or Kate; probably all of them.

He'd felt bad about the calls from Michael that he'd let go to voice mail, even though he recognized the number. There had been two. He had planned to call him back, to give him the courtesy of thanking Stuart for his efforts at the memorial or telling him to go to hell for ruining everything. He knew he should call to ask after the baby, to ask after Gus, but in the end he'd decided there was no point. They hadn't been friends before, hadn't had the time to get there. It had been a near-miss. And while they might have been Elizabeth's husband and son, they were nothing to Stuart. Not now.

What Stuart had missed in family calls, he'd more than made up for in work contacts, though mostly via email. He'd thrown himself into some of the projects he'd been ignoring. Finishing each by crossing the company name off the paper where he kept track of these things with a satisfying squeak of permanent marker. Taking just enough breaks to scan the Internet for the most pressing world news, and more importantly the hottest celebrity gossip.

No, Stuart was getting on marvelously. Depressed people did not have time for celebrity gossip, or so he'd

believed until the morning when there was a knock at
the door, not preceded by an announcement call. One
that didn't fade, even as he pretended with all his might
not to hear it, or the accompanying triad of voices
calling: "Stuart, Stuart honey, are you in there?"

"Stuart Joseph Lewis, I am at you door, and I expect
to be granted entry. Immediately."

"Stuart, open up. We are getting a little fed up with
this, so open up the goddamn door, or I'm going to tell
the super that there's a funny smell up here and come
back with the police."

At this, Stuart sighed and popped up from behind
the couch, where he had hidden himself, even though
the door was solid wood. He walked over, slowly
releasing the latch and tossing an amiable "Hi" into the
concerned faces of his mother and aunts, trying to
make it look like he wasn't barring them entry. Which
he was absolutely attempting to do.

"Well, Glyniss, now you know he's not dead," said
Helen over her shoulder as she pushed past Stuart into
his still sparsely-furnished living room. She stopped
short, saying, "Oh shit. Sorry about that, Stuart. You
know I always end up with my foot in it."

Before he had a chance to say he hadn't been
offended, Agathe stepped into the room, grabbing him
firmly by the arms and saying, "What your aunt means,
Stuart, is your mother, and all of us, have been
concerned about you. You haven't been returning our
calls." She held her cheek up for the requisite kiss. As he
brushed it with his, he realized his stubble had gone
beyond a missed shave, far beyond. He pulled back,
apologetically rubbing at the side of his face as he

watched Agathe follow Helen over to the metal bench in the living room, adding, "Well, you haven't been spending your days decorating, I see."

Stuart nodded before turning to his mother, the only one still standing in the hallway, looking as if she was working up the courage to come inside. He held a hand out for her, to help her over the threshold, and she rushed forward. "We didn't think that you'd…" she murmured into his chest, hugging him tightly enough to demonstrate that was exactly what she'd thought.

"No. I haven't killed myself," he said, wondering once more what it was about him that made everybody think that in a time of crisis that his first thought was always going to be suicide. When Emily had first suggested it, he had been incensed, believing she thought him a coward wanting to avoid life. He realized later that in truth he was a coward. Death scared him shitless, and under no circumstances would he ever take an active part in his own demise, aside from the occasional social cigarette.

"Well, you haven't returned any of our calls," Glyniss repeated, working hard to remove any trace of blame from her voice.

"And you repeatedly ignored us when we came out of our way to check on you," Helen piped in, much less concerned about her tone, her earlier gaffe having done nothing to dissuade her commitment to tough-love tactics in dealing with her nephew.

"I've just been really busy working," he said, noting Agathe's delighted reaction to this response.

"Oh? You're painting again? That's just wonderful, Stuart! What is it that you're working on?"

"Well ummmm. No. I meant work, work. I had

some business stuff to catch up on," he said, watching her face fall slightly. "Have to keep the money rolling in to continue living in this high style," he finished lamely, waving his arm around the room.

"Well, that's something I guess," said Helen, grudgingly impressed that he'd been putting his efforts into anything nearly so practical as paying the bills.

"Well, yes," added Glyniss, her protective instincts pushing away her timidity over arriving unannounced. "That's very important. I'm glad that you are keeping busy."

Agathe said nothing but looked at him in a way that expressed disappointment. No one said anything for a moment, until Stuart finally offered the ladies something to drink, mostly for an opportunity to get a moment to collect himself.

His great-aunt asked for tea. "Not one of those ridiculously overpriced ones full of roots and god-knows-what. A proper cup of tea." Her nieces followed suit. Stuart headed over to the kitchen to plug in the kettle as Agathe called out another request. "And in a clean cup, please, Stuart." The comment struck him as odd until he looked around the kitchen to see a large number of unwashed dishes piled up in the sink and spilling over onto the counter. Funny, he hadn't noticed that before. While the kettle boiled, Stuart fussed around, finding clean mugs and tea bags and hoping against hope that the milk in his fridge had not gone off. It had. He hadn't noticed that either. So Stuart headed to yet another cupboard, thankful that honey doesn't go bad. As he reached overhead for the jar, he caught sight of himself in the shining dome of his espresso maker. Even through the distortion, he could see that he did not look good. His hair was greasy and his face scruffy. He stared a moment, wondering when he had last shaved or showered. As casually as he could, since he could feel the three sets of eyes staring into his back as the women chatted over trivial matters, Stuart dropped his chin to his chest, turning it to the right to determine if he stank. He did. Just a little, but enough. The kettle screeched, causing him to jump, but he didn't reach to unplug it. He was coming to the slow and uncomfortable realization that he wasn't getting on so well after all. And that he was sad. Beyond sad. Stuart's heart was broken.

He wasn't angry or ashamed or scared of winding up alone. He was simply, terribly, heartbroken. And all of the things he had done or not done in the past few weeks to shove it down or out or away had done nothing but delay the hellish moment when he had to face it. This moment.

He didn't hear Agathe come up behind him. He didn't notice she had unplugged the kettle to silence the piercing whistle. He didn't notice that he had started to cry until she turned him and wrapped her arms securely around him. She was stronger than he would have expected. It felt almost as if she was supporting him, and he let her, dropping his head to rest a moment on her snowy hair. Stuart couldn't remember the last time he had been hugged by his great-aunt. It wasn't just the men in his family who found touching uncomfortable. Aside from the perfunctory kiss on the cheek at each greeting and departure, he hadn't really touched his aunt in years.

"I'm not fine," he whispered.
"I know," she said, not letting go.
"It hurts."
"I know."

*   *   *

It was hours before the women left the apartment.
During most of that time, Agathe sat with Stuart on
the hard metal bench, occasionally patting his knee and
barking out orders to her nieces. The sisters reverted to
their childhood selves, running around to make the tea,
do the dishes, sweep the floors and obediently follow
directions, until the place looked pristine, if not
particularly pretty.

Glyniss remained quiet and almost cheerful
throughout, though Helen grumbled enough for both
of them, albeit under her breath.

Glynnis was so relieved to see Stuart freshly shaved
and in such capable hands. Even though Agathe had no
children of her own, Glyniss had always thought her
aunt was a wonderful mother, a better mother than
hers had been, than she herself was. She felt happy to
turn her favourite son over to the care of her aunt, or if
not entirely happy, then absolutely relieved. It was the
best thing she could do for him, letting Agathe take
control. She was best left to busy herself with things she
could not mess up.

Afterwards, after the house was clean and groceries
had been ordered and paid for; after Stuart had
promised to pick up the phone next time, informed
that if he didn't he could expect another such visit;

after the women had hugged and patted and pinched him goodbye, Agathe determined they were in need of a drink.

"I think what I'm really in need of is a chiropractor," Helen moaned as she ducked into the waiting cab and felt her back shout its protest. "Do you know the last time I handwashed a floor? Never, that's when."

"Well, Helen, it was well worth the effort for your nephew's wellbeing, don't you think?" Agathe asked pointedly, after giving the driver directions to an establishment befitting three women looking to have a drink in the middle of the afternoon.

"Of course it was!" Glyniss piped in, almost giddy over how well she thought things had turned out—the burden of the worst-case scenario lifted, her duty done. "I think he is going to be just fine now."

"I don't think a tidy house is the antidote for Stuart, Glyniss," Agathe said flatly, trying to impart some realism in the crushing way those born and raised through wars and depression seem compelled to do.

Seeing Glyniss's face fall, she sighed and softened her tone somewhat as she continued. "True, he looked much better when we left than when we got there, but I feel we are going to have to keep an eye on that boy. He needs an interest, something to occupy his time. I do wish he would start painting again."

"He's not a child, Aunt Aggie," said Helen. "He's a grown man. I mean hell, nobody came and ordered my groceries when I was sick, did they? Not that I'd have wanted them to. That would have annoyed the hell out of me."

"Men are different, Helen," sniffed Agathe, leaning

back in her seat. "You must have started to figure that out by now."

"Oh, that's hooey. He's going through an awful time now, sure. But no to be able to function, come on. Functioning is what being a grown man is all about. He can't have his hand held forever, and he's going to have to learn how to deal with life at some point," said Helen matter-of-factly. Then, catching the scathing glare from her aunt, she asked, "Isn't he?"

Glyniss, her sense of calm and satisfaction gone, could no longer pretend she was ignoring the conversation while looking for mints in her handbag. Dropping it on the floor by her feet to get their attention, she snapped, "How can you say that, Helen? If it were your children we were talking about, you wouldn't be so cavalier." Against all good reason, since Glyniss never won these battles, she went on, "Well, maybe you would. You probably would throw your kids to the wolves, come to think of it. Teach them a lesson or something."

"Oh, you think? Well, maybe I would, but I'll never have to make that choice, because I didn't raise kids that are afraid to face the world."

"Girls," Agathe interrupted, her tone clipped and sharp.

"Stuart is not hiding from the world. The world has been hitting him full in the face in the past little while. If you weren't so heartless, you'd have noticed. And Graham is doing just fine, I'll remind you."

"Yeah, well, don't try and take credit for jobs you didn't do."

"Girls!" Agathe said again, louder this time.

"Why you…"

Glyniss wasn't sure what she was going to say, but

she wanted it to be something she couldn't take back. Something that would noticeably alter the smug look on Helen's face and shake her infuriating confidence, if only for a second. She never got the chance.

"Stop the cab! Stop this FUCKING cab right this instant!"

Glyniss, Helen and the cab driver all started at the shrillness and the volume of it, then again as he slammed on the brakes. He turned to look at them as if to verify he'd heard what he just thought he'd heard. They looked back at him wide-eyed, not sure they could believe it either.

"You two think you are the only ones that can behave like animals?" said Agathe, returned to her natural state of refined power.

"I..." Helen trailed off, not sure of what to say.

"I have had just about enough of the two of you for one afternoon and would ask you kindly to get out of this vehicle so I can return home for a civilized drink and a bit of silence."

"But..." Now it was Glyniss' turn to falter, waiting for further instructions.

"I said get out. And I meant get out. Find your own way home, continue to scream at each other on the street, shove each other into oncoming traffic, I really don't care. But get out of this car. Grown-ups indeed."

Helen silently opened the door. Glyniss followed her sister out onto the sidewalk.

Just as the car started to slowly roll away, the window lowered, and the women were informed, "Just don't kill each other, because I was serious when I said that Stuart will need our help, all of our help, in the next while. God help him."

Watching the cab depart, Glyniss was not sure what she felt. As much as she'd been lectured and advised by Agathe over the years, it had been a long while since she'd been yelled at. And she'd never been dumped out on the street. She wasn't sure what to do, so forgetting her recent desire to inflict irreparable harm on her sister, she turned to Helen for guidance and found her standing with her hands on her knees, laughing.

"Oh, Helen, is everything a joke to you?" she asked, distraught.

"Come on, Glyn, that was funny. I mean, did you hear her? I thought that cab driver was going to have a heart attack. I didn't know she had it in her, to be honest. I guess we *are* related." She stood up and wiped her eyes, shaking with laughter until she had to lean over again.

"I don't think she did it to amuse you," Glyniss said, watching her sister wheeze on the side of the road.

"Oh, don't worry, she got hers. This is killing my back." Then slowly straightening up, Helen asked, "So, are we going to continue ripping into each other, or are you going to flag a taxi?"

Glyniss sighed and timidly stepped onto the road to look for an approaching taxi.

"I'd tell you to show a little leg, but I'm really not sure that would help."

"Oh, shut up, Helen," Glyniss said, but as much as it annoyed her, she couldn't keep the smile out of her voice.

August

Her cotton skirt, thin and rain-soaked, slapped wetly against her thighs as she walked. Her feet were sodden in flimsy summer shoes. The outfit had gone entirely wrong. What was meant to have left her feeling airy and unencumbered had become a clingy, uncomfortable second skin suffocating her as she walked, squelching and sucking past the shop windows full of mannequins, looking so sophisticated and enviably dry.

Kate always asked herself at times like these why it was that she never ever seemed to get things right. As hard as she tried, as much effort as she put forth, things had this terrible tendency to end up screwy. She knew that if Megan was there, she'd tell her that she was not unique in this thinking and not nearly as special in her misery as she liked to think. So Kate was happy that Megan was not there.

As she marched along, shoes smacking at her heels and the pavement with a calmingly repetitive "thwack", Kate slowly started to surrender to the soaking. Once she gave herself up to it, it really wasn't all that bad. She was wet. Very wet. All over, with no dry patches under the arms or behind the knees. She could feel the wet everywhere. It's not so very often that your entire body gets to feel something.

As she succumbed, she argued to herself that the real frustration with wet weather was the unwinnable battle to stay dry. To defend all limbs and packages and pant legs simultaneously was futile and destined to make you feel a failure. However, now that she stood there, head tilted so as to allow the fat droplets to hit her square in the face, Kate felt invigorated, scrubbed clean. Baptized.

Baptized?

Why was it, she asked herself, that whenever her thoughts turned to the greater wonders in the world, above farce or fashion or sarcastic commentary, religion was only a thoughtbeat behind?

Thoughtbeat!

She repeated it to herself, thinking about what a delightful word it was. She marvelled at the descriptive qualities of "thoughtbeat" and wondered how it could be that it wasn't even a word at all. People were forever tripping from one idea to another. It didn't take a moment, or a second. It was obviously a thoughtbeat. How could people explain this mental phenomenon any other way? How had she?

Then Kate swore, because she had walked into a newspaper box on the side of the street, and she'd done so with a noisy and painful crash. Then she swore again when she realized she was about three blocks past the subway entrance she had been shooting for, which meant she had spent at least the last ten minutes lost in her own thoughts and had no recollection of the journey. That kind of thing was always happening to her.

She checked herself over, determined there was no

damage and debated briefly whether it would take less time to walk back towards the last stop or keep heading towards the next one. Her original destination was closer, but in the end it really didn't matter, since she was already soaked to the bone and could probably use the exercise. She started walking again, losing herself almost instantly in images of fluffy towels and large glasses of wine.

She had just about convinced herself that buying a bottle for herself on the way home was important for fighting off any possible chill and not a sign of the onset of alcoholism when Kate swore again, having just bumped into something else.

Turning a sharp corner, she'd come face to chest with a man out walking his dog and had hit him hard enough to taste wet cotton before bouncing back.

"Oh, god, sorry about that," said a youngish voice before adding, "Calm down. Calm the fuck down."

"I'm fine, I'm perfectly calm," said Kate, pulling herself up to full height, offended by his words and tone. Too bad, because he was pretty good-looking. Made sense to her, since the good-looking ones were almost always assholes.

"No, I was talking to the dog," the stranger said, pointing to the little clump of wet fur clawing up the side of his leg.

"Oh. Oh, right," Kate said, looking down at the sad little rat.

"Name's Edna," the young man told her. "The dog. The dog's named Edna."

"Oh. Yes. Right," she said, again wondering what the hell had happened to her speaking abilities. She looked up at him, feeling stupid, and seeing the string of damp hair hanging limply in her eyes, which she assumed looked terrible. Kate decided it was best just to cut and run, so offering a shrug by way of excuse, she was about to start off when the young man spoke again.

"I'm Simon."

"Oh. Right. Simon." Then, just to ensure that he thought she was some kind of simpleton, she added, "Simon and Edna."

What the hell is wrong with you? She thought furiously, trying to remember what was actually supposed to come next in this type of conversation.

"And who have Simon and Edna nearly knocked flying?" he asked with a bit of a smile on his face.

God bless him, thought Kate once he'd opened the door.

"Oh, right." Oh, Jesus. "I'm Kate."

"Nice to meet you, Kate," said Simon, sticking out his hand. "Sorry again about bumping into you."

"Oh, it's fine, just a hazard of city living I guess," she sputtered, amazing them both with an articulate sentence. Deciding it best to leave on an up note, Kate gave a slight head bob and started to walk away when she heard something quite extraordinary.

"Hey, listen."

She stopped dead in her tracks, a bit like a startled deer. She knew what this was; she'd been hearing about incidents like this her entire life, though she'd never experienced it herself. She was about to be asked out on a date, by a stranger.

If TV and movies are to be believed, chance meetings are the main way the species is propagated.

You go to the coffee shop, the movie house, the subway station, and catch the eye of some man who can't stop himself from plopping down next to you to make enough friendly conversation to get your number. You have date one, two, ten, thirty, move in, get engaged, have a baby, and the world stays its course to overpopulation and demise.

Kate did believe in TV and the movies, though god knows why. She had never been approached by a man, well, any sober man, and invited on anything resembling a date.

"I don't mean to hold you up..."

Until now. She turned slowly, one hand flying to her hair while the other slapped blindly at the streams of mascara she could taste as they made their voyage from eyelash to chin. She could not believe she was about to be asked out on a date just like the girls from *Sex in the City*.

"...but my friend told me there is a great museum around here."

And he's freakin' cultured too! she thought, a smile breaking across her face as she nodded at him encouragingly.

"And I've been wandering around looking for it for like half an hour. Do you where I can find it?"

Son of a bitch. He wasn't asking her out on a date. He was asking her for directions.

Now, this wasn't new to Kate, as people were always stopping to ask her for directions. She answered them all cheerfully, and usually quite accurately. But this particular request, after such an obvious date-like build up, was not to be welcomed or tolerated.

She planned to seek her brand of gentle vengeance

by telling him she no idea where the museum was (which of course she did), so she was surprised to hear herself say, "You can't bring a dog into a museum," in a tone reminiscent of her mother's.

"No. I know. I was going to…"

"Leave Edna to sit outside in the rain?" she said, a little appalled at herself.

"Well, er, it wasn't raining earlier when we headed out."

"Well, it's raining now," she said, deciding that anyone who would leave a dog out in the rain deserved to be treated like a dirtbag.

"Yeah, yeah, of course," Simon said, and Kate was delighted to see him looking so sheepish.

"Well, whatever. The gallery's two blocks north of here and one block to the east, you can't miss it," she said, heading on her way before turning around to say, "At least get her a bag or something to cover her while you're browsing."

"Yeah, yeah, of course," he called after her before correcting himself, "I mean no. No. I'm not going to leave her in the rain. I'm not going to go at all," he said, watching Kate's back retreating up the street.

"Hey, Kate!" he yelled, and even though it was still raining and she was annoyed, she turned around.

"Hmmm."

"I just wanted to say, despite Edna and the rain thing and the swearing, I'm not a jerk, you know."

"Uh-huh."

"No, I mean it. I don't usually yell. I just wasn't expecting a downpour and whatever. I'm sorry. I'm sorry I bumped into you, and I'm sorry about the dog and…" He trailed off, shrugging while he stood there in the rain. Something about they way he fiddled with the leash and looked down at the sad little puppy made Kate say, a bit shyly, "Yeah, well, I'm sorry I told you the museum is two blocks north of here, because it's actually about half a block south."

Simon smiled, his eyebrows popping up for a second as if to say "well played". "Oh. Right. Well, good thing I'm not going there then." He gave her a little laugh and tossed the hair out of his eyes.

Then Kate felt it again. That feeling. She knew it. He was going to ask her out. More than that, she was going to say yes. And they were going to be together forever and ever and this was going to be the hilarious anecdote about how they met that they would tell at their wedding and the weddings of their children. She knew it as sure as she knew she would take her next breath and stood waiting for it, but you know, trying not to look to eager.

"Okay, well, nice meeting you, Katie."

Oh, and he had called her Katie. "Yeah, nice meeting you too, Simon," she said happily, waiting for the invitation to follow.

"Okay, come on, Edna, let's go."

"Bye, Edna," Kate said with a little wave. Any second now. He was really building up the suspense.

But as he turned around and started walking, she became somewhat less certain that he was planning to ask her out. She was so shocked by this turn of events that he was nearly down the block before it sank in. He had turned the corner by the time she'd picked up her phone and dialed Megan's number, ready to rail against the fates that taunted her so mercilessly.

By the time Megan had picked up, listened to the tirade and asked her, "Why the hell didn't you ask him out, if you thought he was so great?" Simon was well and truly out of sight. "For fuck's sake, Katie, if you think this is the guy you are going to marry, you should have asked him out," Megan spat into the phone, apparently in a tough-love mood.

"But…"

"Oh, I don't want to hear it. It's not his job. It's not his choice. If you want to see him again, go make sure you are going to see him again. How hard is that?"

"But…"

"No buts about it. You are not a goddamned princess. He's not a failure for not asking you out first. Stop waiting for other people to do the dirty work for you, or you're going to spend the rest of your life alone and bugging the hell out of me."

"But he's gone now," Kate finally managed to say.

"Did you see where he went?"

"Sort of."

"Well, stop wasting time, and go see if you can catch him."

"I already am," she said as she realized she was turning the same corner she'd seen him take a few minutes before.

"Well, woman, there may be hope for you yet," Megan said, pleased with this turn of events and becoming instantly more companionable. "Do you see him?"

She didn't. The street was so empty, she could hear the echoing drum of the rain on the pavement. She was for one second as devastated as the occasion called for. The missed opportunity, the pouring rain now starting to make her shiver, the deserted city streets. To be alone like that even for a moment in a city of millions was an eerie feeling. The whole thing was tragic and romantic, and she let it wash over her, enjoying the poetry of it. But she didn't stay that way for long. She couldn't shake the little jolt of nervous energy bouncing through her body. The kind that makes your fingers tap or your knee shake the dinner table. Something that told her she hadn't lost him. He was just misplaced.

"No, I don't see him," she told Megan, starting down the street again. "But I think I'm going to keep looking."

* * *

The year she left, Stuart hadn't gone out much. He'd opted instead to lie low, drink a lot of vodka and actively avoid getting himself entangled in anything remotely resembling a career.

So it was no different than the years preceding it. Except that he had spent a good deal of his time in that year trying to figure out how that could be the case. Emily had been the girl he was going to marry. Not because he had to, or felt she wanted to or because he didn't know what else to do. He was going to marry her, because he loved her. She was the one piece of his life that he knew was meant to be. Except, as it turns out, she wasn't. The problem had eaten up a good deal of his free time in that year.

Why?

He had come up with an answer. Stuart determined that the reason why his life had gone on after Emily was because it might have been love, but not real true love. But this neat little surmise was tossed out the window in the tortuous weeks after Elizabeth died. So he had then turned his energies towards finding a new answer that could possibly explain how, now that the real and absolute worst thing he could imagine had happened to him, to Elizabeth, the same damn thing had happened again? What did it take to make life stop?

After he'd opened up to the remaining women in his life, and to himself, letting the magnitude of his sorrow sweep over him, he had expected to fall again, this time without looking forward to it as his due. A reward for having a bad thing happen to him, for being the victim. This time he was terrified he would fall so far into the blackness that he wouldn't be able to get himself out. But it hadn't happened that way. Even after that, there had still been work to do and shows to watch and food to eat—still mail to open and family to deal with. And the more he talked about it, the more he wanted all of those things. One day, when Graham called to leave what had become a typical check-in message on his machine, Stuart had picked up the phone. Then, during one of those calls, when Graham had made his familiar suggestion that they go out for a beer, Stuart said yes and went out and enjoyed it.

He found himself slowly becoming aware that other people's lives were still going on too, so when Kate had called him one day, looking for a new ear to bend about her run-in with Simon, he was willing to listen.

"So you didn't find him then?" Stuart asked her as

they sat at The Local, sipping on pints as she told him how her story of love at first sight had become the story of the one that got away.

"Of course I didn't. There are like a million little streets downtown, and it was pouring rain. I spent like twenty minutes shouting 'Edna, here Edna, here girl,' like a retard, and then I went home. Then I actually typed Simon and Toronto into the online directory and thought it might be possible to track him down, until I realized you can't even search the directory without a last name. I know. Super lame."

"Ah, that's awful Katie," he said, though he couldn't help smiling. "I'm sorry."

"Oh, well. You know, it's all right. I'm fine."

"Hey, you are allowed to be pissed about it. That blows," he said. "Trust me, I'm not a huge fan of the stiff upper lip, as my recent emotional tailspin can attest."

"No, no, that's not it. I am actually fine. I mean yeah, yeah, I wish I had caught him. But I didn't, and I'm bummed, but I'm also fine. I don't know." She twisted her glass, making overlapping wet circles along the table. "It occurred to me the other day that I really don't have all that much to complain about at the moment. I know, I know. When I told Megan, she almost fell right over too, so don't look at me like that. Of course, I CAN complain, it's just if I really think about it, I am not spending all of my time feeling all that terrible. It's weird. I don't really know why that is."

Stuart looked at her for a minute, determining whether he knew her well enough to tell her the theory that had been percolating in his brain since he'd decided to climb out of the hole Elizabeth's absence had left in his life. He took a long drink, figuring if he was ever going to know her any better, he was going to have to start telling her this kind of thing. To show her how the rusty machinery of his mind really worked.

"Well, I get what you mean. And I think I have an answer for you."

"Oh, really?" she said, crossing her arms as she leaned them on the table. "Do tell."

"I don't know. You may not want to hear it, it's not really pretty."

"Well, life never is, is it?"

"Okay then. So I have been giving some thought over the past little while to how it is that I, Stuart Lewis, having had what many would consider one shit year; losing the love of my life, twice actually; my house; possibly my mental faculties for a time etc… etc…am really no different sitting here with you this August night than I was one year ago when I still had all of those things. How is it that, after all of that, I'm still sitting here, drinking the same beer, wearing the same clothes and happy to hear that they are playing The Band on the stereo."

"And?" she said, urging him to continue.

"And, the answer I have come up with is; it's because a broken heart won't kill you…and, Kelly Clarkson be damned, it doesn't make you wiser or stronger either."

"Huh," she said, leaning back in her chair to give him a long look. She said nothing more, so he continued.

"It's not the end of a relationship that will ruin you. Or in your particular case, having it end before it's started. It's a defect in personality that will ruin you. A split just offers you a golden opportunity to shine up your character and take it on the public sympathy tour. It gives you a sense of entitlement, a license to let all your bad bits run free. And some people just have a lot of bad bits."

Kate furrowed her brow. Realizing that he was not being cute, or shooting the shit, she wished she hadn't been drinking, which made her body heavy and her brain slow and fuzzy. He was actually talking to her, and she was worried now that she wasn't up for the challenge. Still, she didn't want him to stop talking, so she just nodded at him, hoping he couldn't tell.

He continued. "So, for example, if your true love leaves and you end up leading an emotional support group, it's because you like to be in charge. If you have been cheated on and end up taking out all of your anger and resentment on the next person you date, it's because you are an asshole. If your best friend dies tragically and unexpectedly and you start shooting heroin into your eyeballs, it's because you've always had a secret desire to give it a go. The truth is, Katie, like it or not, people don't change. Some may want to, or think that they should. A few may even be able to make a great job of faking it, but it's rare. And it's sure as hell not brought on by affairs of the heart.

"So if you end up unable to function in society any longer, it's because you are weak. And as much as I have always been afraid of finding it out, I've been tested this year. It turns out that I am not weak. And neither are you.

"We sit here feeling sorry for ourselves because we haven't lost our minds out of grief, because our lives are lonely. We act cheated that we haven't gotten our fair share of agony, or of the utter bliss we are supposed to feel when something goes right in our lives. We sit here thinking every emotion should be accompanied by some kind of orchestral swell, and we aren't doing it right, if we are just plugging along, living a life and fucking getting on with it. But, and I can't take all the credit for this, Elizabeth has told me this before, that IS life, and we are doing it right and to ask for more is like asking to be an emotional basket case or a manic depressive or something, and it's ridiculous, and I'm going to try not to do that any more, because it is all a huge lie."

Kate didn't know what to say. It was a lot to take in, and not the kind of conversation she was used to having with Stuart, with anybody really. It was making her feel like an adult.

"So you really believe all of that, Stuart?" she asked.

"To the very depths of my banged up, blackened but still beating heart," he replied.

"Jesus, maybe you *are* growing up," she said, almost to herself before giving him a little smile, just at the corners to show she wasn't making fun, and pushing her glass towards his until she heard it clink.

*　　*　　*

Stuart sat on a particularly sunny Saturday morning, a hammer in one hand, awaiting the arrival of those who still loved him. It was a small group by some standards, a crazy one by many. In his other hand, he held a weighty frame encasing a drawing of the girl he had loved most in the world, even if by most standards it wasn't the right kind of love. A drawing he'd worked on for hours, trying to capture everything he thought he'd miss about her as the years went by, and his brain got full of worries over mortgage payments and proctology appointments. The things about her he was terrified to lose.

It wasn't the cleanest thing he had ever drawn; you can't help but end up with some sloppy bits when you are pouring your whole soul into something. Passion like that can't stay within the lines, nor should it.

It was his aunt who had told him, when he'd shown it to her, that it was the best thing he'd ever done with the talent God had given him. And it was his mother who had told him it was okay for him to keep this little piece of her for himself even if it would be a fitting gift for someone else, someone who might have needed it even more than Stuart. It was his brother who had said to him that it was about time he had something to put up on those bare walls. Which is why he was now wandering the rooms of his house, trying to find a comfortable place for Elizabeth to hang out in his apartment.

The place had begun to transform in the last few weeks after Agathe had decided that Stuart needed a project to get him thinking about the future and enlisted a crew to get him started. What began with a few furniture website links sent to his email account had grown into dinner-time planning sessions and weekend shopping excursions, involving all of the women in his life, most more than happy to spend his great-aunt's money and pray to their inner Marthas for inspiration.

There was now a proper couch, a dining room table and the things that a woman's touch bring to a place, namely candles and picture frames. It was as he was unpacking the frames that he realized that he did not have a picture of Elizabeth to put in any of them. All of those years and all those emotions, and not even a damn Polaroid. So he'd taken a canvas and a sharp lead pencil, closed his eyes for a moment and started drawing.

He gave the walls a final scan before deciding she'd be happiest above the television, where she wouldn't have to watch all the crap TV he watched and where he could, just every once and a while, have a little chat with her.

While nowhere near as handy as his brother, Stuart managed to measure and insert the correct plug into the plaster and hang the frame straight, so she'd be ready to greet everyone as they came to eat pizza in celebration of his thirty-fourth birthday and witness what Kate had irritatingly begun to call "the final reveal" of their collective work.

As he waited for the first knock at the door, Stuart wasn't happy. This did not worry him, though, as it might once have. Because the other life lesson Stuart had extracted from the past twelve months, so different from all of the others yet not so different from them, was that the opposite of happy is not unhappy. Not a lot of people know that.

There is this theory, this Snopes-worthy belief, that if you aren't happy you must be miserable, and need to immediately sign up for a course, or buy a book, or go speed dating or to the psychiatrist, since you are incapable of getting happy under your own steam. And to be not happy means you have failed and your life is a big, glorious, wasted mess.

But it's total crap. You can be unhappy and still feel content. Feel content or safe or cozy or lucky or proud or all or any of the above in combination.

It's not that Stuart wasn't aware that happy was good. Happy was the preferred state of being. He wasn't anti-happy. If you happened to be one of those people breezing through your life as happy as the day is long, Stuart would say more power to you.

It's just he no longer subscribed to the cult of happy. He couldn't. He had learned that being happy is not essential to a satisfying life.

This is not a terrible thought. It's one to be celebrated, shouted from the fucking rooftops if you think about it. The pursuit of happiness has been the ruin of many people and turned even more into real sons of bitches.

So at this particular moment, on this particular day, Stuart wasn't happy, but he was content. He had regrets about things unsaid and undone and paths not taken, just like the rest of the world. And he had days where he missed his best friend so much that it took his breath away. It was a pain searing but satisfying. Complete. Something that, for all of the aching that he'd done for Emily, he hadn't felt before. A pain he knew he would feel again. It was good, though. It was real, a real hurt that proved something to Stuart that he'd always been desperate to know: how much he was capable of loving someone. He knew now. Infinitely. He had it in him, and that was enough.

Acknowledgements

My thanks to Allister, Sylvia and everyone at Darkstar for making this a truly rewarding experience.

Love and endless gratitude to my parents, Pam, Jim, Sean, Erin, Kevin and Dan for their constant support and encouragement

Special thanks to my friends who inspire me by living their lives so fully...but always leave time for a pint and a laugh (and the occasional interpretive dance).

Finally my thanks to the gifted educators who helped me fall in love with stories, and to those who taught me how to tell them (thanks Dave!).

Photo by Alex McKee

Kerry Kelly is a native of North Bay, Ontario.
She holds a Bachelor of Journalism degree
from Carleton University and has been a full-
time professional print and web writer since
1998, covering a broad range of political,
economic and social issues in her writing career.

She likes both the Rock and the Roll, and
while she has yet to call Toronto her home,
she's happy to admit she lives there.